and snot to ice. I still have nightmares… Ah, cold is cruel!" At last the witch stopped speaking and bent her head. Plaits of black hair curtained her wolfish face. The only noise was the swoosh of waves caressing the wooden hulls of the outriggers. This silence had not happened before.

Has she finished? The prisoner tried not to hope – not even in this small thing.

The woman roused from her memories. For the first time that day, she looked her victim in the face. With a thrill of horror, the girl once again saw her captor's strange eyes – red irises in a sea of bloodshot white.

The witch spoke: "I was a child, weak and small, but I vowed that some day I would destroy those who had banished me to that place!"

The girl shivered. These words were new! Something told her they were important. Dread battled curiosity.

The witch's gaze shifted and, though she stared at the prisoner, she did not seem to see her. "And I will," she muttered. "By the breath of the Salamander, I swear it!" The red eyes refocused. "It would have been easy to die, to give up. Do you feel that?"

The girl did not answer.

"Yes, I thought you must." The woman chuckled, an unlikely noise. Razor-sharp fingernails tickled bamboo bars. "I grow almost fond of you. I have never told anyone the story of my childhood, and you are so attentive." The Fire-witch draped an arm round the girl's cage. "Imagine that child, sent to die alone on a frozen rock. Imagine yourself in my place. Would you have found the strength to survive? Would you have hated enough to go on living?"

Against her will, the girl felt the long-ago child's terror as her own. She too knew loneliness. "Why would anyone do that to a little girl?"

"They feared me!" The voice grew harsh. "My own people. Some fool of a seer spun a lying tale when I was but a Seven-year. Said I was dangerous … that I would destroy the Balance of All Things."

The prisoner drew a steadying breath. So it had been foreseen – this war between the Elemental spirits! The war she had been supposed to stop. She hugged herself, feeling the sharp bones beneath her skin, bones that still ached with growing pains. She was too young, too ignorant and untried. Was it any wonder she had failed?

"But still," continued the Fire-witch, "the Elders of my island feared to kill me themselves. Instead, they banished me to a rock on the edge of the western sea. There the ground is sharp with frost year-round, and the waves carry ice like spears."

The girl had seen the witch kill without mercy – had stood over the charred remains of her victims. Even so, the woman's tale played out in her mind's eye. She saw a seven-year-old girl standing on a frozen rock in the middle of a lonely sea, watching a boat vanish over the horizon.

Her heart spoke before her mind could stop it: "Didn't your parents try to save you?"

She had said the wrong thing. The woman's expression grew so terrifying that the girl gabbled question after question: "How long were you there? How did you finally escape? Did someone rescue you?"

Heartbeats measured the interval of danger. At last the witch regained colour. "I was there through the monsoon – half a year of torment. Escape was impossible. Even if you survive the cold, even if you bash enough limpets from the rocks to keep from starving, the sea ice imprisons you on that place. A swimmer would be cut to shreds long before the cold of the water could kill them."

"But you did escape in the end. Did you make a raft?"

"From what? Rocks? Nothing but sere-grass grows there."

Deep in the witch's pupils, fire flickered. The captive said: "Someone must have rescued you." She was ashamed to hear her voice shake.

"The Salamander." Red-lit eyes watched. "It Chose me before I was born. My banishment was a test. I proved worthy, and the Fire spirit set me free."

The prisoner's heart pounded. She too had been Chosen before birth by an Elemental.

"Don't you want to know how the Salamander rescued me?" The woman grabbed the cage, pressed her face against the bars. Her prey flinched, and the witch opened her mouth in a silent laugh. Red lips drew back to reveal white and oddly pointed teeth, and the girl thought of the hungry mouth of an anemone.

The woman let go, leaned back, still smiling. "The sea around my piece of rock was shallow. The Fire spirit caused lava to flow again from the volcano that had given birth to the mini-islands there. Molten rock boiled into the sea for days upon days. When it was done, there was a path across the waves. The Salamander's gift smouldered and spat flame and ash, too hot to touch and survive – but I could not wait. I walked barefoot over the burning bridge!" The witch's face became, for a moment, that of an enraptured child. "And I was unharmed! I may bathe in fire and take no hurt. The Salamander is my mother and my father!" Her eyes shone. Their pupils erupted with the red-black of seething lava – miniature volcanoes – and the girl's mind emptied of everything except terror.

"I walked across the burning bridge to the nearest inhabited island and was greeted as a god by the people who lived there. Because they feared me, they gave me all that I demanded. A boat loaded with supplies. Clothes made from the finest cloth – red silk. I never wear anything else. Red for fire, for the Salamander. Red for revenge! Soon … soon!"

Long-nailed fingers reached, clenched the bars until the knuckles gleamed. The Fire-witch shook the cage. She was incredibly strong. "I could kill you now."

The captive froze. She didn't hold her breath – she simply couldn't breathe.

"Incinerate you as you cower there. So easy…"

"Why don't you?" Almost a plea.

"When it is the right time." The witch rose to her feet in a sinuous movement and strode away with a flourish of scarlet silk.

As soon as she was out of sight, a small orange monkey emerged from a coil of rope and scurried across the tilting deck. It carried a half coconut shell in one hand. The creature crouched beside the cage and pushed the shell through the bars. It held a few mouthfuls of water. She took it eagerly and sipped the warm, fishy-tasting water, trying to make it last. The sun beat down on her cage from dawn to dusk, and she was always thirsty.

"Thank you, Scoundrel," she said. The monkey reached through the bars and stroked her arm. Its touch was so comforting that she had to fight back tears. The cling-monkey's huge amber-orange eyes never left her own, almost as though it was trying to tell her something. She smiled at its mournful face and wondered how it managed to find food for itself, let alone water for her. Why did the Drowned Ones tolerate a pet monkey on their raft town? Whatever the reason for Scoundrel's survival, she was grateful. Every day since her capture the monkey had come. Its daily visit was the one thing that gave her hope.

Nine days a prisoner of her most hated enemies, the Drowned Ones. Nine days squashed inside a cage on one of the hundreds of outrigger canoes roped together to create the pirates' raft town, only let out morning and night to use the privy bucket. Nine days without magic, without a sign from any of the three Elemental spirits who had Chosen her as their human champion in their war with the Salamander – a war

8

that would determine the fate of the Balance of All Things, and therefore life itself.

The witch visited her daily, drawn by some fascination the prisoner could not understand, for she was no longer a threat to the Fire Elemental or its agent. The Dolphin and Albatross had abandoned her. Worst of all, the Tortoise was gone too. She felt the Earth spirit's absence like an aching hole, almost as big as the one left by her mother's death.

The cling-monkey made a soft cheeping noise, reminding her to drink.

As she swallowed the last mouthful, a figure rounded the corner of the canoe's hut and the girl looked up to see Nim, the Drowned One boy.

An old and fierce hatred rose at once. It was Nim's fault that Dain, her mother, was dead. The boy had been shipwrecked on her home island, Yanlin. She had saved his life and hidden him from her Elders, who would have killed the pirate boy on sight. In return, he had set half the town on fire and helped his people invade her island. She had defeated the Drowned Ones in the end, sinking a raft town in the harbour and sending the remaining two scuttling back to sea, but her mother had been killed in the battle.

Storm hated Nim for betraying their friendship and

ignoring the life-debt he owed her, but now she felt a shameful relief that he had come to see her at last. For nine days she had seen no human beings except the Fire-witch and the guard who brought her privy bucket. Isolation was part of her punishment. So what had changed? Was she about to find out what her enemies had in store for her?

He looked different from the boy she had saved on Yanlin. A year older and taller, of course. But more than that … there was a confidence that had not been there before. Nim had not let the witch kill her nine days ago. He had seemed to be in charge of the other Drowned Ones, but that could not be true. Nim was a mere youth, newly Chosen. He would be the most junior of apprentices. His Elders would not let him decide her fate, for she was their greatest enemy. She was the Weather-witch of Yanlin.

"Hello, Storm," said the pirate boy. "We need to talk."

2

"Why should I listen to anything you have to say?"

"The Elders want to see you, but we need to talk first."

"They're wasting their time. The Elementals have abandoned me. I have no magic."

"I know you believe that, but I don't." Nim squatted on his heels, eye level with her, his freckled face annoyingly calm. The monkey immediately darted to the boy, climbing on to his shoulder.

So Nim was the reason the pirates tolerated Scoundrel! Storm's eyes grew hot. It was stupid to feel jealous, but the cling-monkey was her only friend in this place. She watched the tiny creature wrap a confident arm round her enemy's neck before turning to gaze at her with huge eyes. Usually, she could tell what Scoundrel was thinking. Not now.

He's only a monkey, soothed her mind-voice. But he wasn't. Scoundrel was the Tortoise's emissary.

"Trust the spirits. Trust yourself." Nim was watching her too. The boy and the monkey – two pairs of amber eyes wearing the same patient expression. Old eyes, ancient, knowing.

"Earth!" she breathed. "You were Chosen by the Tortoise!"

"More than Chosen. The Tortoise made me an Earth-witch."

Her stomach twisted. *How could this be? How could the Tortoise…?* Her mother, Dain, had also been a Child of Earth.

Storm was once more holding her mother's dead body, looking into the familiar face made strange by death. The Tortoise, beloved spirit of the Earth, had sacrificed Dain for a Drowned One! For this sea-cursed pirate, who had killed her mother as truly as if he had struck the blow. *Why?* To prevent war between their peoples? But there was still war! Worse, there were signs that the fighting between the Drowned Ones and Islanders was about to get so bad that the Salamander – who fed on hate – would grow strong enough to break the Balance of All Things. Nothing had changed. Only

Nim lived and Dain did not.

Scoundrel leapt down and ran to her, thrusting his hand through the bars of her cage. His warm fingers gripped her goose-pimpled arm. Storm shivered with rage. "Earth-witch? *You?* Why a—"

"Filthy Drowned One? Do you think the Elementals never grant my tribe the favour of magic? You Land Grubs!" Nim surged to his feet. "Arrogant, privileged—"

The boy cut off his tirade and grimaced. "Look at us? See how easily we fall into the old patterns? If we do not learn a new way the habit of hate will kill us."

The truth of his words drained her resentment. She had flared up so quickly. It had felt good to be angry, to have someone to blame. Nim knelt in front of her cage. His face was inches from hers, his amber eyes insistent. "Why anyone, Storm? The Elementals Choose, not us. Look, I have kept away since your capture because my Elders suspect that my loyalties were affected by … my experiences on your island. I have managed to convince them to keep you alive for now, but I don't know how much longer I can do that. We need to work together, you and I—"

Work together? What did Nim want from her? Before he could explain, a new voice intruded.

"Work together how, young pirate? You and yours work for me. Don't forget it!" A familiar figure emerged from the shadow of the hut.

Storm gasped in surprise. The woman's face was unmistakable: broad cheekbones sliced in two by a knife of a nose, nostrils quivering as though sniffing for profit. *Waffa? Here?* For a heartbeat, Storm wondered if her captivity had addled her brain. But she wasn't seeing things. The woman advancing on them was the tally-keeper of the Pact – the Fifteen Families that were the hereditary rulers of Bellum Island.

Head of one of the aristocratic families, Waffa kept the trading accounts for the island. The last Storm had heard, the tally-keeper had been maneuvering to oust the Pact's leader, Talon, and take charge of the island herself. What reason above or below seas could Waffa have for being here?

Rich and fortunate Bellum, called the belly button of the word because of its location in the middle the Inner Sea, controlled trade between the islands. The Pact's Fifteen Families had grown rich by extorting unfair taxes from the less powerful islands. In the past few generations they had even begun to steal from their own people, impoverishing the common folk and setting their island on a course for revolution.

Storm quickly realised that Waffa's bid to lead the Pact must have failed. Whether from fear of the coming revolution, or a simple desire for more power than the Pact was willing to grant her, it seemed that Waffa was actually working with the pirates to betray her island!

Nim shot Storm a warning look. The Drowned One boy jumped to his feet and turned to face Waffa, confidence in his every movement. He was almost unrecognisable as the desperate boy she had rescued last year. But then, Nim was no longer a No-thing, an orphan and social outcast. He was an Earth-witch, arguably more important than his Elders, or even the Pact's tally-keeper.

"We work *together*, Mistress Waffa," Nim said firmly. "We Drowned Ones will take our share of the spoils of Bellum. You would do well to remember that."

Waffa huffed, then shot a calculating look at Storm. "And *you* would do well to remember that this girl is an unknown quantity. Her power might win Bellum Island for us, but only if we can control her. If we can't, she is better off dead, as the Fire-witch desires."

"Of course." The casualness in Nim's voice made Storm's skin crawl.

Fool! she berated herself. She had actually begun to let herself believe the pirate boy wanted to help her.

"A nine-day in the cage should have persuaded the Weather-witch to work with us," Nim said. "My Elders wish to speak to her. I will take her to them."

"And I have come – with your Elders' agreement – to make sure she does not trick you." Waffa beckoned. Two Drowned One warriors suddenly appeared, moving towards them a few canoes to Storm's right. They advanced quickly, leaping across the wood and rope bridges that connected each canoe to its neighbours, like so many threads of a cobweb.

The warriors, a man and a woman, dropped lightly on to the deck of her canoe and moved forward until they stood behind Waffa. They carried bows on their backs and long knives at their hips. Their eyes fastened on Storm's face, and she saw both fear and hatred.

"I have no magic," she said. "I cannot hurt you."

"I hope, for your own sake, that you lie." Waffa barely glanced at her. "In any case, it is best to make sure." She attempted to draw back the bolt that secured the door of Storm's cage. It stuck, and the tally-keeper swore and thumped the door. Scoundrel growled low in his throat and the tally-keeper kicked out at the animal, nostrils flared with anger and contempt. The monkey yelped in pain. Before she even knew what she intended to do, Storm was up and out of her prison, slamming the half-open door into Waffa. "Leave him be!"

The tally-keeper staggered back across the narrow deck. The woman tripped and, with a shriek, fell headlong into the narrow sea-space between one canoe and its neighbour. All was confusion. Scoundrel screamed from Nim's shoulder, where he had taken refuge. "Don't shoot!" shouted Nim.

The Drowned One warriors had bows drawn, arrows notched and aimed. Storm was a heartbeat from death. Nim grabbed her arm and tugged her behind him. The warriors swore, but the bowstrings slackened. He had saved her life.

Why was Nim shielding her? Storm struggled to think. She felt lost in a fog of exhaustion and fear. *He must want something from her – something important enough to take such risks – but what could it be?*

"Fish the Bellumer from the water!" Nim ordered. "Now, before she gets sucked under."

The tally-keeper was still shrieking. She must have grabbed one of the ropes tying the canoes together, for her screams kept pace with the raft town.

The warriors glanced at each other. The woman shrugged. "I'll fish her out." She slung her bow on her back and loped to the side of the canoe. Her male companion watched, still wary, as the female warrior leaned down an arm and heaved, dragging the Pact's tally-keeper wriggling up the side of the canoe like a fat oil-fish on a line. Waffa grabbed hold of the gunnels with both hands, hooked a leg over the side and swung herself aboard. She dropped heavily to the deck, crouching on hands and knees, spluttering.

When she got to her feet, Waffa's nose was a white shark fin protruding from a red face. Her long, greying hair was plastered to the sides of her head like a seal's pelt. She glared at Storm, who knew she had made a life-enemy.

"Bring her!" spat the tally-keeper.

"You can leave that to me," Nim said in a carefully calm voice, keeping eye contact with the other Drowned Ones. "Escort Mistress Waffa to the Elders. She isn't used to our raft-town paths, and I wouldn't want her to have another mishap on the way."

After the merest breath of a hesitation, the male Drowned One nodded curtly and held his hand out to Waffa. "Come, Mistress. I will help you over the ways. Your pretty shoes are wet and slick now."

"I don't need help! I am perfectly capable … and I told you to—" The tally-keeper squeezed water from her dripping hair in frustration and looked down at her sodden shoes. Ruined, shapeless and slippery. "Oh, very well." And with a last, murderous look at Nim and Storm, she sloshed and slid after the guards.

3

Storm and Nim made their way to the centre of the raft town. After nine days squashed inside a cage, Storm could barely stand. She stumbled in and out of canoes, wobbled across swaying rope bridges.

The raft town rose and fell with each breath of the sea. The decks of the canoes were crammed with wooden huts and screens. Boxes, barrels and firkins were everywhere, piled higher than her head. It was impossible to see where she was going. Everything stank of seaweed, fish guts and tar.

Scoundrel twined himself round her shoulders, grumbling in her ear. She was glad she didn't speak Monkey. She would rather not know what the animal thought was about to happen. She knew what *she* thought. Her legs began to shake, and it was no use pretending it was because of the cage.

No great plan miraculously presented itself. Escape was not an option; her body was barely functioning, she had no magic, and she was alone in the Inner Sea on a Drowned Ones' raft town full of enemies with a Fire-witch who wanted to fry her to ash.

Storm crossed yet another swaying rope bridge and saw a tall platform bobbing in front of her, lashed to canoes along all four sides. She had seen this before; the pirate raft towns were built to imitate the lost island homes of the Drowned Ones, with a mini-mountain of wood constructed at their centres, like a dormant volcano. In the middle of the platform sat a large building – the seat of power on this floating town – the hut of the Elders. A flag on its roof billowed and cracked in the wind. It showed a face with a gaping round mouth: the symbol of the hunger of the Drowned Ones. Hunger, Nim had explained, for land of their own.

Four people waited beside the hut. The chief Elder was a short, powerfully-built woman with iron-coloured hair. Storm remembered that her name was Peggot. Her brother had been captain of the raft town Storm had sunk in Yanlin harbour. He had died on that day, along with many of his townspeople. Peggot, Storm knew, wished her dead.

The other Elder was a grasshopper of a man, with a stooping back and hands clasped together as though praying to the Ancestors. Waffa, hair and sodden clothes dripping, stood nearby. To one side, more terrifying than all the others combined, waited the Fire-witch. Storm's heart began to pound in her chest. She knew she must die, but being burned alive was a horrifying prospect.

Don't be so foolish, said her mind-voice. *They won't risk the raft town catching fire. They'll drown you.*

Nim pushed her forward. Storm bent her head slightly, her face wooden. She would not show her fear. Ma might be watching from the land of the Ancestors, and Storm wanted Dain to be proud of her as she faced death. "You wished to see me, Elder Peggot?"

The woman's face was stone-hard. "Has your time in the cage persuaded you to come to an agreement with us, Weather-witch?"

The male Elder poked his head further forward and rubbed his hands harder. Waffa's sour expression became expectant. Storm looked from one to the next, suddenly feeling more exasperated than afraid. Could these people not hear the truth when told it? Did they think she was lying when she said she had lost her magic?

They want to believe you are their key to the treasures of Bellum Island, said her mind-voice.

But not all her captors were blinded by greed. She met the Fire-witch's eyes; the woman smiled and her long fingers twitched.

"I could not agree to your wishes even if I wanted to," Storm told Peggot. "I speak truth when I say I have no magic!" She pointed to the Fire-witch. "Ask her. She knows!"

"Rekka?" Peggot turned to the witch, an uneasy deference in her manner.

"It is true and not true. The Weather-witch believes what she says, but her magic is merely dormant." Rekka's eyes narrowed as she considered Storm. A cruel smile slowly stretched her lips. "But enough of this! You play a dangerous game by keeping the girl alive! Better to kill her and have done. I and your young Earth-witch can conquer Bellum Island without her help. Kill her, I say!"

4

The Fire-witch's fingers twitched with a murderous desire.

Elder Peggot frowned at Rekka's words, but her eyes were cold as she studied her captive. Storm's breath caught in her throat; the Elder would love to have an excuse to kill her!

Nim stepped forward, confronting Peggot. "The Fire-witch lies! She serves her master, not us. Rekka knows that the Tortoise will not ally itself with the Salamander! The Fire spirit seeks to end the Balance and reign over the world alone. If you put Storm to death, I cannot help you invade Bellum."

"Cannot or *will* not?" asked the Fire-witch with a snarl.

"It amounts to the same thing," said Nim, and Storm

held her breath. She had just learned that he was very brave – if the Fire-witch had been safely on land he would be a pile of ash right now – and that he was fighting for the Balance too! She was no longer alone.

"Your first loyalty is to your tribe, Earth-witch!" snapped Peggot. "Do not forget it. As for you, Rekka, we fished you from the Element you fear most when you were near to death. You owe us your life and will do as we say or the Dolphin can have you again!"

Terror flickered in the Fire-witch's eyes for the merest breath, then she shrugged. "Bah! As you wish."

Elder Peggot snorted and turned to face Storm. "Weather-witch, I agree with Rekka. We have caged you for a nine-day, which would break most to our will. You are either a stubborn liar or your Weather magic is merely dormant and will awaken in extreme need. So I've devised a little test. If I'm wrong … well, you owe me a death, Storm of Yanlin." The Drowned One Elder bared her teeth in a shark's smile. She turned to Nim. "Chain the Weather-witch to the canoe and sail to the appointed rendezvous. The Bellum ships are nearly here!"

At the word "chain" Storm's stomach seemed to flop over. So she was to drown, like Da. The Dolphin would not spare her – she had failed the Elementals.

"Look after Scoundrel for me," she said to Nim, holding out the wriggling cling-monkey. "Promise to keep him safe!"

Scoundrel grumbled and muttered as boy took him.

"I promise," said Nim.

The monkey twined his long arms round the pirate boy's neck. Throughout the twisting journey to the edge of the raft town, the animal's large mournful eyes never left Storm's face. A guard followed them, carrying a heavy iron chain. It clanked at every step.

Storm shivered, thinking of the cold weight of it round her waist, dragging her down to the bottom of the sea. *I will drown and my body will be lost, like Da's, and my spirit will never find its way to the land of the Ancestors.* Would their spirits somehow find each other? Then it hit her: *I'll never see Ma again!* Dain would wait in the land of the Ancestors for the husband and daughter doomed to roam the earth forever as ghosts. The thought was devastating, and Storm stumbled and would have fallen if the guard had not grabbed her arm and wrenched her back to her feet.

At last they arrived at the edge of the raft town, where a small canoe waited, bobbing gently on the waves. Nim turned, and the knot of fear in Storm's stomach twisted tight as she saw that the pirate boy's confidence had finally deserted him. The orange freckles strewn across his face stood out starkly. His jaw was clenched with determination, but his eyes held defeat.

"We have been circling Bellum Island since we took you," he said. "It lies a day's sail to the east. Three of the island's harrier ships have been following us the whole time, spying, waiting for an opportunity to attack. You will be set adrift in the canoe, without oars. We will watch from a safe distance. The Bellumers will take you for one of us – they will assume you are part of an ambush. They will attack you." Nim scowled at her, suddenly fierce. "If you do not use your magic, you will die! Our people are under orders not to save you." His eyes searched her face. Scoundrel gave a low moan.

Storm looked at the boy, at the monkey, seeing the Tortoise in both pairs of amber eyes. She longed to hear the gravelly voice of the Earth spirit once more in her mind, but there was only silence. That was her answer.

"Then I die today."

Nim's face grew even paler. "I see you believe it. I pray to the Ancestors that you are wrong." He jumped into the canoe and motioned for her to follow. The guard shoved her forward.

Her mouth dry, Storm half stumbled into the canoe.

Nim motioned for her to sit on the rowing bench. When she had done so, he took the chain from the guard. Storm sat, as unmoving as the dead, while the pirate boy fastened one end of the chain round her waist and the other to the bench on which she sat. Her heart was trying to pound its way out of her chest.

The Drowned One rose to his feet. He gave her a quick searching look, then leapt back on to the raft. The moment Nim turned away, her fear exploded. Storm bit her lip to stop from crying out.

"Goodbye, Storm," Nim said in a gruff voice. He bowed quickly, still scowling, then turned and walked back towards the centre of the raft town. Scoundrel, perched on his shoulder, watched Storm until they were out of sight.

The guard studied her, stony-faced, as the raft town sailed away, slipping over the cresting waves until it was out of sight.

5

Loneliness came, cold as the ocean depths.

The canoe rose and fell with each breath of the sea, circling on its anchor rope. To the north, she glimpsed three Drowned One war canoes riding the waves. Nim would be in one. Was Scoundrel still with him?

It was so strange that this was how it would end. Would she really never go home again? Never again see Cousin Minnow or Auntie Briathe? Or Teanu, her beloved teacher? This, then, was the fate of those who failed the Elementals. *Ma!* Storm prayed. *Help me to be brave!*

The canoe bobbed, turning Storm to face south. Her eyes scanned the water. Immediately, she spotted them: sails red as blood. One … two … three ships darting in and out of sight, like petrels playing among the waves.

Storm's stomach squeezed tight. The Bellum harriers were coming.

The scarlet triangles grew rapidly bigger as they sped towards her. Now they were joined by one more, and four blood-red sails skimmed the whitecaps. Nim's spies had been wrong. Bellum Island had sent four harriers.

The fourth vessel was approaching from the east. The captain had set the top as well as the main sail and both were fat with wind. The ship was making speed and would beat its comrades to her. She heard a distant bell ring out. Shouts tumbled across the waves towards her, blown by the wind. Almost as one, the three original Bellum ships unfurled their top sails until they too were straining before the wind, gathering speed, as though chasing after the fourth ship.

And then Storm realised that the three harriers *were* chasing the fourth ship. Her canoe rotated on its anchor rope and she saw that the Drowned Ones' canoes had edged closer. She could see figures standing up in two of them, as though trying to get a better view. And then she rotated again and was once more looking at the race between the Bellumers.

Storm's heart began to thud faster. Who was in the fourth ship?

The ship grew ever closer, and she saw that it was

not a harrier after all. It was smaller – a nimble, low-slung vessel – and it was flying across the water faster than any ship Storm had ever seen. Three figures stood on its deck, one hunched over the tiller, the other two crouched in the bow. The boat leapt over the waves towards Storm's canoe.

"Faster! Faster!" she shouted. She had no proof that the mystery ship was a friend, but that possibility was her only chance. The three harriers were chasing it down like sea-eagles after a gull. She could see people moving about on their decks. "Faster!" Storm screamed again, longing for her old magic, frantic to help them.

How do you know they are friends? her mind-voice objected.

"They *are* friends. I know it!" she shouted. "Be quiet and let me hope!" She could see the standards of the three Bellum harriers, but the smaller boat carried a flag that Storm had never seen before: a white narwhal on a black background.

That's a pirate flag, said her mind-voice. *They heard about you in Bellum and want to steal you and offer you to the highest bidder.*

Storm's heart sank. Not a rescue. Still, it was better to take her chances with a pirate than be stuck full of Bellum Town's arrows.

And the Drowned Ones? Will they just stand by while the privateer carries you off?

"Be quiet!" she ordered her mind-voice as she squinted at the approaching boat, trying to make out the faces of the sailors. There was something wrong with them… A chill ran down her spine. Each pirate wore a black mask over the upper parts of their faces. *Why would pirates need a disguise? Who were these people? And what did they want with her?*

The wind strengthened from the south and the chasing ships bore down on the strangers, seeming to leap over the water. The harriers would win the race: they were nearly in shooting distance of their prey. A battle bell rang clanged out, and a dozen arrows rose into the air and plunged into the rippling wake just short of the sailing boat. The archers were testing the distance. The next flight of iron-tipped shafts would be deadly.

Storm tugged impatiently at her chain, watching the approaching sailing boat and the three masked figures. They were almost certainly about to die. Then it would be her turn.

One of the pirates stood upright. Black tunic billowing, the stranger raised something to their lips. Storm caught a snatch of music, the whistle of a reed flute. At the very first note, the wind snapped around, veering to the south with a suddenness that caused the sails of the pursuing ships to collapse. The three harriers yawed wildly, wallowing, suddenly becalmed. A second black-clad figure on the sailing boat rose to its feet and raised both arms overhead.

Storm yelped as her canoe lurched into the air on the crest of a rogue wave rising out of nowhere. The sea writhed beneath her. She gripped her bench tight with both hands and looked for a sign of the Dolphin or glimpse of the Albatross. Nothing. The Elementals still hid themselves from her eyes, but she knew she had just witnessed magic!

Hope returned so violently it took her breath away. *The elderly Earth-witch, Linnet, and his band of witches gathered on Bellum. Had they come to rescue her?*

Her canoe plunged and leapt like a tuna fighting the hook. The sea churned. Tall waves rose from the depths and surged towards the Bellum harriers. Their crews were struggling to trim the sails, but they could not control them in the howling gale.

Storm held her breath as the first of the magicked waves crashed into the leading ship, tossing it like a cork. One after the other, the sea pounded the three harriers. Near to floundering, wallowing like beached seals, all three ships turned back and beat an unsteady retreat south towards the safety of Bellum harbour, tattered sails and pennants streaming in defeat.

Wind and waves still chased the ships, but the seas around Storm grew placid. The fluting Air music stopped and her canoe steadied. The stranger craft sailed directly for her. Its crew were watching her now, eyes invisible behind mask holes. The sailing boat swept to within a rope-throw of her canoe.

"Catch!" shouted one of the witches, and hurled a coil of rope to her. Storm caught it and secured the rope to her bench with a half hitch. The other witch leaned over the side with a hooking pole, grabbed the anchor rope and cut it through with a single slash of a knife. Storm didn't bother to check what the Drowned Ones were doing. Their rowers would already be powering the war canoes towards her, determined to prevent her escape.

"Go!" she shrieked.

The black-robed figure at the helm was already leaning hard against the tiller. The slender sailing boat lurched, swivelled like a striking snake and, with a tug that nearly unseated Storm, leapt across the waves eastwards, dragging the canoe after it.

A deadly wooden rain plunged into the water between

the boats. Storm flinched: too close! A handful of arrows struck the deck of the sailing boat, just missing the crew. The sound of a reed flute rose once more above the waves. Twisting and twirling in the breeze like a gossamer thread of spider silk, Air music floated up into the sky.

The wind shifted, howling in her ears, sending her hair streaming back. The captain of the sailing boat remained bent over the tiller, fighting to ride before the storm. The two witches knelt at the back of the vessel, facing the pursuing sea pirates. The shorter of the two raised his hands, and the waves rose at the gesture, as though a leviathan rose from beneath the sea.

Storm's canoe rode high on the swell then sank into the trough. She turned, shivering, blood thrilling through her veins like ice, and watched as the monster wave, speeded by the force of the magicked wind, rose higher and higher, until it obliterated all sight of the pursuing Drowned One war canoes.

Storm almost shouted with glee at the idea of her enemies –her mother's murderers – tangled in weed at the bottom of the sea, their bodies eaten by fishes until only gleaming white bones remained. Then she remembered Scoundrel … and Nim. His words rang in her head: *See how easily we fall into the old patterns? If we do not learn a new way the habit of hate will kill us.*

She waved her arms frantically at the two witches. "Don't drown them! They mustn't die!" But the wind blew away her words and the monstrous wave surged after the war canoes. "Please," Storm prayed to the Ancestors, "keep Scoundrel safe!" A breath of hesitation. "And Nim!" Then Storm forced herself to continue. "I beg of you, Ancestors, for the sake of us all, save the Drowned Ones!"

Wave and storm dwindled from view and Storm slumped back on to her bench. She was helpless to change whatever happened now. The sailing boat ploughed through the sea ahead of her. Its three occupants seemed to be conferring. Watching them, Storm wondered where her rescuers were taking her, and what would happen once they arrived.

6

A magicked wind propelled her rescuers' ship over the waves. Its black flag, emblazoned with a white narwhal, cracked and rippled in the wind. Land appeared on the horizon – a small rocky outcrop that grew rapidly larger. The ship cut through the water with a precision that signalled a master sailor at the helm.

She studied the mysterious *Narwhal*'s captain – it could be anyone. She would soon know who they were and why they were taking her to an uninhabited scrap of rock. They had reached shallow water, but the ship leapt forward as eagerly as ever – its captain seemed intent on grounding them! Storm braced for impact.

At the last moment, the captain leaned hard on the tiller, and the ship veered to the right, dragging the canoe in its wake. They circled the island, and

Storm spotted a tiny bay where four ships bobbed at anchor. Standing on a thin strip of beach, watching their approach, was a group of ten or twelve people.

The skipper of the *Narwhal* shouted an order. One of the witches lowered the sail while the other dropped anchor. The captain grabbed the tow rope and hauled the canoe to the side of the ship. All three of her rescuers jumped down into Storm's canoe.

The tallest of the witches took off his mask. "Hello, Storm." It was the grey-haired Air-witch from Bellum Island. He smiled down at her and she felt her breath loosen. Linnet, the elderly Earth-witch who was helping her battle the Salamander, had sent her rescuers! The other figure removed his mask to reveal a young Water-witch who was another of Linnet's people.

"It is good to see you both again," Storm said, feeling suddenly shy. She didn't even know the men's names, yet she owed them her life. "Thank you for rescuing me – Did Linnet send you?"

"Yes. The Balance has never been at greater risk. The Salamander does not rest!"

"I… There is something I must tell you." Storm looked away from their friendly faces in embarrassment. How would they feel when they found out that the Elementals had taken back their magic and she was no longer a witch?"

"Enough talking!" barked the skipper of the *Narwhal*. She – for the voice was a woman's – squatted in the bow of the boat. The two men either side of her began to row. Storm's heart beat harder as spray stung her face and the smell of seaweed and sand filled her nostrils. She had not stood on the earth for so long. Suddenly she longed to be ashore, to feel land beneath her feet.

With a judder and a crunch, the hull scraped bottom as the canoe grounded a few strides from the beach. The skipper stood and threw a rope to one of the waiting men, then the masked woman and the two witches jumped out of the canoe and splashed ashore. In a heartbeat the little boat, still carrying Storm chained to its wooden bench, had been dragged up on to the shingle. It immediately tipped to one side, and she sprawled, chain clanging, into a tide-waste of smelly seaweed. Storm scrambled to her feet with difficulty, the chain making her awkward, aware of all the eyes watching.

"Get her loose!" ordered the skipper.

An older woman strode forward, pulling a file from her waist bag. "Please," the woman said politely. "Hold your hands behind your back while I file this hasp." The woman set to work with an expert's skill. Her hands were strong and calloused.

A Maker, Storm thought. *Blacksmith or silversmith.* She studied the others gathered to meet them on the shore of the small islet. Although she didn't recognise any of the faces, no one looked hostile. She glanced at the skipper of the *Narwhal*, who was watching the progress of the file through the iron impatiently. The woman took off her mask.

"Mer!" Storm stared at a tall girl who gazed back at her with clever, calculating eyes. She had been rescued by Waffa's own daughter! Storm knew that Mer hated her mother. The older girl had rejected the aristocracy into which she had been born and joined a group of Bellumers who, tired of the greed and corruption that meant ordinary people grew ever poorer, intended to overthrow the Pact. Did Mer know that Waffa was conniving with the Drowned Ones? Had she rescued Storm to get back at her mother?

The smith grunted as the file bit through the last bit of metal and the chain fell to the ground with a clunk. Storm hardly noticed. She could not take her eyes off the girl who had once tried to kill her and nearly succeeded. Whatever else she might be, Mer was *not* her friend!

"Why did you rescue me?" Storm asked. "Who are

these people?" She glanced at the smith, who had stepped back to join the other strangers, all dressed in black. The two witches stood to one side, waiting.

"We are the Rebellion, Weather-witch," Mer replied. "Those who fight the Pact and its greed. I spoke of them to you before."

"I remember."

"I offered you the opportunity to work with us. You chose not to."

"My fight is with the Salamander," Storm said. "I am no friend to the Pact, but civil war on Bellum must be averted or the only winner will be the Fire Elemental!"

"So your friends believe." Mer gestured at the two witches. "Tell her," she ordered.

The Air-witch raised a greying eyebrow. Mer had the arrogance of the Pact bred into her: she was rude without even being aware of the fact. "Greetings, Storm of Yanlin," he said with a polite bow. "Linnet, the Earth-witch, sends his regards. It is good to see you safe once more. It is time we were properly introduced. My name is Zephyr. My colleague is Fountain." The young Water-witch bowed in greeting.

"As you know," Zephyr continued, "Linnet has gathered a group of witches on Bellum to fight the Salamander. The Fire spirit desires a war between

41

the Drowned Ones and Islanders so it can grow stronger. A war so devastating and violent that it will enable the Salamander to break the Balance between the Elements at last. Linnet believes that only you can defeat the Fire-witch. He also hopes that you and the Drowned One Earth-witch, Nim, can work together to prevent the coming war between the pirate clan and the Islanders. So when Mer approached us with a plan to rescue you from the Drowned Ones, we readily agreed. And her plan has, against all probability, worked." He nodded with calm courtesy to the older girl, but Storm sensed a reserve.

"Didn't you wonder what Mer stands to get out of this?" Storm asked.

"Mer claimed friendship with you as her motive," Zephyr explained. "That didn't fit our knowledge, but we decided we had no choice but to accept her offer. You are too important to the war against the Salamander not to take the risk."

Storm winced. She would have to tell them soon that she had lost her magic! She frowned at the older girl, her sense of unease growing. "Why gamble your life in a dangerous bid to rescue me from the Drowned Ones, Mer? Not out of friendship. We both know how much your friendship is worth! What do you get out of it?"

"You are about to find out." Mer pointed at the two Bellum witches. "Take them!"

Before the Air-witch could put his flute to his lips or the Water-witch raise his hands to call the sea, nets were thrown over the two men and they were hurled to the ground and bound in rope-like parcels.

"What are you doing?" Storm lunged forward, but someone grabbed her by her hair and flung her to the ground. In a heartbeat, Mer was kneeling on her chest. The Bellumer pulled a long knife from her belt and pressed its edge to Storm's throat.

"I do what I must!" panted the older girl. "We all seek revenge on those who have wronged us. And I need you, Storm, Weather-witch of Yanlin, to deliver my enemy to me!"

7

"Try to use your magic against me, Storm, and I will kill your friends! I don't intend to hurt them; I just don't want them to interfere."

Storm hesitated. Best not to confess her lost magic until she knew Mer's plans. "Let me up. I won't attack."

"I saw you fight the Fire-witch, Storm. I know what you're capable of. But if you give me your word to behave nicely, I'll let you up."

"You have my word."

The knife was withdrawn. Storm rose to her feet, watching Mer and thinking frantically. The Bellum rebel had always been impossible to read. Mer was unpredictable – except for her undying hatred of her mother, who had killed her own husband, Mer's father. Figuring a way out of this mess would not be easy.

The witches wriggled inside their bindings like giant caterpillars. Storm sensed their frustration and alarm.

"Take them back to Linnet," She said. "Once they are safe, I'll help you."

"You're not in charge, Storm." Mer smiled sweetly. "They will remain as my hostages until you help me destroy my enemy." Her voice was as gentle as her smile, but Storm was not fooled.

"Your enemy? Do you mean Talon?"

"Not Talon. His fate is sealed, as is the rest of the Pact. He will answer to the Freedom Tribunal once we hold the island. You are going to help me avenge my father's death. You will deliver Waffa to me!"

"Your mother?" Storm's mouth fell open in surprise. "But she is with the Drowned Ones!"

"I know."

"Do you expect me to fight a Drowned One raft town single-handed?"

"You've done it before, I understand. Do you doubt your power?"

"No…" Even to her own ears, her voice sounded uncertain.

"Don't worry. I know you have an odd dislike of killing. I'm not going to ask you to fight the Drowned Ones. I need them as allies in my war on the Pact. You have the wrong idea entirely. You aren't the hero of the story, Storm, but a mere playing piece. I'm going to trade you for my mother."

Storm felt her mouth fall open. Mer had rescued her from the Drowned Ones only to hand her right back to them! She was to be bartered, like cargo, for Waffa. Storm had no doubt what the tally-keeper's fate would be.

That, said Storm's mind-voice, *is only the beginning. Once Waffa is dead, Mer will join forces with the Drowned Ones and go to war on the Pact! And the Salamander will grow strong enough to break the Balance!*

A chill surged through Storm's blood. Was this it? The event she had been Chosen to prevent? Linnet had warned her that all-out war between the Drowned Ones and Islanders, death and violence on a horrific scale, would strengthen the Salamander. The Fire Elemental fed on hate. A world war would make the Salamander so powerful that no one would be able to stop it boiling the seas dry.

"You can't!" Storm stared at the older girl, appalled, knowing nothing she could say would change Mer's mind. The Bellumer was a non-believer. "You don't understand!"

"What don't I understand, Storm?" Mer was relaxed,

her expression cynical.

"You can't help the Drowned Ones attack Bellum Island! The war won't stop with Bellum. You know that all the islands would send fleets to protect trade. We would see fighting and death in every sea and on every island! All that hate and violence would feed the Fire Elemental – make it strong enough to finally destroy Water once and for all."

Storm studied Mer, searching for any sign that the other girl understood what was at stake. "Don't you see? The Salamander cares nothing for life! It hates the perpetual truce between the Elementals. Fire wants dominance at all costs. I promise you, if you do this, you will break the Balance of All Things! You will help the Salamander to boil the seas dry!"

Mer's people began to mutter and exclaim. But the rebel leader simply raised a disbelieving eyebrow. "That old fable? I told you, Storm, I don't believe in the Balance. I'm not at all sure I even believe in the Elementals. We humans make our fates."

"How can you not believe? You yourself saw the Fire-witch incinerate two of Talon's guards."

"Oh, I believe in the power of magic – as a born talent, not the gift of a spirit."

Storm shook her head in despair. "As someone who

was given that gift by three of the Elementals, believe me when I say you are wrong! I have seen them, spoken to them!"

"I'm sure you think so." Mer shrugged. "I may be mistaken. Perhaps Elemental spirits exist. Perhaps all magic comes from them. I don't, actually, much care."

The older girl bared her teeth in an icy smile. "I shall punish my mother for her crimes against my father and against the people of Bellum Island. Then I will wage war on the Pact. I need the help of the Drowned Ones to win that war, so … I will use them. The only 'balance' I care about is that between right and wrong, between the oppressor and the oppressed. And I will put that balance right or die in the attempt!"

Storm wanted to scream at Mer. Why could she not understand? Instead, she said, as calmly as she could, "Your hatred of your mother blinds you. Do you really think you can trust the Drowned Ones? They have their own ideas of right and wrong, oppressed and oppressor. They won't share Bellum with you, and you are a fool if you think they will!"

"You're mistaken, Storm. I and I alone can give them what they want: islands to live on. Other islands, of course, *not* Bellum. I believe you come from a small island in the second sea. Yanlin, isn't it? That's the sort of place I have in mind."

It took Storm six stuttering heartbeats to understand what her ears had just heard. Mer, defender of the oppressed, intended to betray every island except her own! The Drowned Ones would put every woman, man and child they captured to the sword. The Island race would be wiped out!

"Would you really cause so much suffering?" Storm asked.

Mer shrugged. "A few islands. A handful, twelve or thirteen. It's a small price to pay for peace between our peoples."

"Peace? What will happen to the people who live on the islands you give to the Drowned Ones?"

"They can find new homes. We will share them out between the islands that remain to us."

"And will Bellum take many?"

"Bellum? Why should we? The islands I have chosen are in the second sea, far away from here. No, it will be the responsibility of the islands in the first sea to give refuge."

"You are as selfish as the rest of the Pact!" Storm shouted. To think she had once liked this girl and wanted to be her friend! "The Islanders of Yanlin will never surrender their homes. None of the Islanders will. You know that. They will fight, and the Drowned Ones will kill them all. I can't let you do this, Mer. The Elemental spirits will not permit it!"

Only one thing could stop Mer now. Magic. Her old magic. Maybe now, at this crucial moment, the Elementals would relent. She knew she had to try.

Please, Albatross! Storm prayed. *Give me back my magic so I can stop the Salamander. I beg of you, Dolphin, help me defeat your enemy! Tortoise, do not abandon me! I am trying to do your will!*

Her eyes searched the heavens for any sign of the Albatross; her ears strained for any hint of Air or Water music. The taste of defeat already in her mouth, Storm tried to sing. Her voice was tuneless and sour. Desperately, she stretched out her arms, seeking a single note of the lightsome music of Air.

"Stop it, Storm, or I will kill you!" Mer raised a hand, and her archers drew their bowstrings and aimed a dozen arrows.

"Why do you still deny me?" Storm shouted at the sky. Defeated, she looked at Mer with tear-filled eyes. "Now you know. The Drowned Ones will not want me! I am useless. The Elementals have taken back their magic."

Mer gestured for her archers to put away their

weapons. Her hand shook and she drew in a long, deep breath before she spoke. When she did, her voice was as gentle as ever. "So it seems. Happily, your problem will not affect my plans. The Drowned Ones are bound to think you were the one who called the wind and waves and sent those harriers scrambling for home. By the time they find out you are no longer a witch, it will be too late – Waffa will be dead! And I have other witches I can use against the Pact."

"They will never help you!"

"You forget those two." Mer gestured to the bound witches. "With them as hostages, your friend Linnet will do my bidding."

The prisoners lay motionless upon the ground, listening, watching. *What did they think of her now they knew she was no longer a witch?* Head bent in shame, Storm did not struggle as her hands were bound in front of her and she was tugged back to the canoe at the end of a rope.

←——————→

Mer sailed the *Narwhal* with two crew: a woman in her thirties and a younger man. They raised the mainsail while their captain sang softly to herself as she piloted the ship out of the harbour. The *Narwhal* was soon snaking through choppy seas. It was a perfect day for sailing – the sky clear, the sun's heat cooled by a steady easterly.

Storm was tethered to the mainmast. She leaned against it, watching Mer at the helm. The mast's wood was hard and unyielding, like Waffa's daughter herself.

She felt out of time; soon the journey seemed as if it was the only thing that was real and would go on forever, with no beginning and no end. It was oddly peaceful. She would not mind if she sat here forever – watching a mad woman sail them across the sea.

Mer stopped singing. Her eyes fastened on something and an exultant smile flickered over her face. She ordered the woman to slacken the mainsail and turned to the man who was watching them both. "It's time!" she said with a glance at her captive.

The man drew a wicked-looking knife from his belt and advanced on Storm. She cringed as he squatted next to her, showing her the knife's sharp blade and grinning. Did Mer mean to kill her after all? But the Bellum girl ignored Storm, the man and his knife. She stared eastward, holding the ship steady as it floated on the waves, waiting, like them, for the arrival of the Drowned Ones.

8

Silent as sharks, five war canoes darted over the waves and surrounded the *Narwhal*. A few pirates manned the oars, while the rest stood with bows strung and drawn, iron-tipped arrows aimed at the crew of the *Narwhal*. At this distance, they would not miss.

"Don't fire!" Mer shouted. "I come to barter!" Hand resting lightly on the tiller, long braids snaking in the breeze, the rebel daughter of the Pact radiated confidence as she faced the Drowned Ones.

Storm could not help being impressed. Mer seemed oblivious to her own danger. A familiar screech rose into the air. Scoundrel was perched on Nim's shoulders, his long tail lashing in agitation. The Drowned One boy sat in the prow of the lead canoe. He motioned to the archers to lower their bows. "You are in no position to barter!" he shouted. He was the youngest of his party, but there was no question that he was in charge.

Mer nodded at the man squatting beside Storm. He grabbed a fistful of her hair, twined his fingers through it and forced her head back. She screamed in surprise and pain. Fear leapt like a frog in her belly as the edge of a blade pressed against her throat.

"I have the Weather-witch, Drowned One!" shouted Mer. "If you do not do as I say, my man will slit her throat."

Storm, staring at the sky through tears of pain, listened to the sound of wood upon water, the clink of tackle in the wind.

Nim spoke at last: "Harm her and you'll have an arrow in your own throat before you can take another breath!"

In answer, the man yanked her hair, forcing her head further back. Her neck felt like it would break. To her fury, she heard herself groan in pain. Storm clenched her teeth to keep from crying out again. She could see nothing but the blue expanse of sky. Would the grey specks of gulls riding the thermals be the last thing she saw in this life? When Nim spoke again, she was almost sick with relief.

"Perhaps you should tell me what you want." Nim

sounded defeated, but Storm was not fooled. The Drowned One boy was at his most dangerous.

She held her breath. Nim was clever. She knew he wanted her alive, but he was up against an opponent just as clever as himself, and even more ruthless.

"What I want is to help you!" Mer laughed, and the reckless glee in her voice made Storm shiver. "I have come to give you the Weather-witch of Yanlin! You should thank me!"

"Why return the witch to us?" Nim's voice was disbelieving. "You stole her in the first place!"

"I needed a bargaining chip. You have something I want. Give it to me and you can have the Weather-witch."

There was a pause as Nim took in Mer's words. Then: "What could we lowly, dispossessed ones have that you would want, Bellumer?" The scorn in his voice was hot enough to curdle eggs. "You're a filthy Land Grub! Doubtless one of the greed-maddened Pact. You already own everything!"

Mer ignored his jibes. "You carry a criminal on your raft – a traitor and murderess. Give me Bellum's tally-keeper. Give me Waffa!" The desire in her voice was brutal and unquestionably sincere.

Silence. Storm watched the seagulls spiral overhead.

They had come closer, drawn by the hope of fishing scraps. She listened to their screams, the only sounds punctuating the ever-music of life at sea – the thud of waves beating against hulls and the answering creak of wood and rope. The man's grip on her hair was relentless.

"What is Waffa to do with you?"

Storm heard reluctance in Nim's voice. He had been taken by surprise and didn't like it.

"That is not your concern, pirate! Give her to me and I will release the witch to you. Otherwise, we leave as we came, and you will never see Storm again. Try to stop us and she dies!"

Storm's scalp had gone numb, but her spine screamed from being bent backwards so long. Her ears rang; her heart thudded unevenly. The flat of the blade pressed against her gullet, making it hard to breathe. She wondered how long she could last before she either fainted or became hysterical.

After what seemed an eternity, Nim replied: "I cannot make this decision alone. I must speak to my Elders."

"Then run along and ask the grown-up what to do, little Drowned One. I will wait. But don't be long. Storm is looking a bit green."

Somewhere, beyond her vision, there was the faint

splash of oars. A gentle current rocked the *Narwhal*. Time had gone to sleep.

Storm opened her eyes, not aware of having shut them, and saw the shadow of an enormous wingspan circling high above her. The Albatross! It had come to save her, to claim her again. Tears welled, trickled itchily down her face. She blinked and the shadow was gone. She had fooled herself. Storm slipped back into a half-faint born of exhaustion and terror.

A stony voice roused her. One she recognised too well.

"Well, Islander, I am the Elder, Peggot, and I have brought Waffa. Before we hand her over to you, I want to know why you want her so much you have risked death twice over. And what you intend to do with her!"

"The woman is a murderer!" The loathing in Mer's voice roused Storm completely. She groaned, and the man loosened his grip, allowing her to straighten her neck slightly. Now she could see the scene unfolding in front of her.

Waffa stood an arrow-throw away, behind Peggot. The tally-keeper's face was pale with fear. "Mer!" cried her mother. "You cannot do this. I know you are a class-traitor, but even you cannot betray your own flesh and blood."

"Like mother, like daughter, I guess." The older girl's face hardened into a ghastly smile. "Why are you here, dearest Ma, if not in order to betray the Pact and so make yourself even richer? My father's so-called treachery is a mere wisp of sea foam compared with your perfidy!"

"I…" Waffa shook her head, but the fear and confusion in her face condemned her.

"What will you do to her, if I hand her over?" Peggot asked again.

"Nine years ago, this woman falsely accused my father of stealing from the Pact. He was put in a canoe without food and water and set adrift far from land. I think the punishment should fit the crime, don't you?"

"N-no!" stammered Waffa. "You can't mean that! I didn't… It wasn't my fault… Mer! I'm your mother, for Ancestors' sake. Have mercy!"

"Oh, I will," Mer said. "The same mercy you gave to Da!" Her face twisted, made ugly with hate. "I want to see her in a canoe! No paddles! No food. Water for three days, to give her time to think about her end. NOW! And then, Drowned Ones, you get your Weather-witch."

Peggot frowned thoughtfully at Mer, who shrugged, suddenly calm.

"No hurry," said Waffa's daughter. "I have been waiting nine long years to avenge my father. I want to savour this moment. Although your Weather-witch is not looking too well."

Storm saw all eyes shift to her. All except Waffa, whose face seemed to be melting in terror as she stared at her daughter. "Don't listen to Mer!" she gabbled. "I can give you Bellum Island, not her! I can give it to you without the witch. I have powerful friends—"

"Who you will betray like you betrayed my father?" snarled Mer. "You won't get the chance. Well, Elder Peggot? Will you fetch a canoe, or shall we see how much blood a Weather-witch holds?"

Forced to decide, Peggot shrugged. "You can have Waffa. We would have killed the Land Grub anyway once she had served our purpose." She gestured at a warrior. "Fetch one of the small canoes!"

"No!" Storm's shout of protest emerged as a tiny squeak, but Peggot still heard it.

"You have something to add, witch?"

"Mer is lying to you. I have no magic! She's cheating you."

"Do you *want* to die?" Peggot laughed in disbelief. "Why would you tell such an obvious lie? Your magic all but drowned our war canoes!"

"That wasn't me. It was two other witches. Mer has taken them captive too."

"Indeed." Peggot shook her head contemptuously. "I don't know what game you think you are playing, Weather-witch, but I should save your breath."

"This isn't about me, or the tally-keeper, or Mer. Killing Waffa will give the Salamander even more power! Look at his Fire-witch!"

Rekka stood to one side, swaying, fingers twitching, her face luminous in triumph.

"What is that to me?" asked Peggot, barely glancing at the Fire-witch.

"Ask me again when the seas are boiled dry!" Storm rasped. "The Elementals are at war. The Balance is threatened!" Once more she tried to sing, tried to find a hint of Air magic or Water magic. But her mind was empty. Storm managed a pitiful croak. She stared at Peggot through tears of despair. "See? I have no magic. Isn't that proof enough? Mer is cheating you."

Doubt flickered across Peggot's face.

Through a haze of tears, Storm saw Nim. His shocked face said he believed her.

"Clever Storm!" said Mer. "I don't think she enjoyed her time as your guest, Elder Peggot. Rest assured that she lies! It was she who magicked the wind and waves when I helped her escape."

"It is true that the Weather-witch has not lost her magic!" Rekka said. "I would know. Make the trade. Storm will be far more useful than the tally-keeper." All the time she was speaking, Rekka stared at Storm, and the look in the Fire-witch's eyes sent cold shivers through her blood.

Peggot's face cleared. She gestured to her warriors. "Set the Land Grub adrift!"

Mer and Rekka had won. The Fire-witch smiled slyly at Storm. Helpless, she watched Waffa struggle with a Drowned One guard before being tossed into a small canoe. She listened to the tally-keeper's wails as the canoe was towed out to sea. Mer stood motionless, watching the two canoes as they swept over wave after wave into the distance and out of sight.

"Your mother is as good as dead," Peggot told her. "Now, fulfil your part of the bargain … or die."

Mer's eyes reluctantly left the path of her mother's boat. She shivered, then turned and strode across the deck towards Storm and her captor. "Give the knife to me!"

The man let go of her hair. Storm gasped in relief as the pain stopped. She rubbed her neck, staring up into Mer's face, trying to read her destiny. The older girl hefted the knife, examining its finely honed edge. She met Storm's gaze and gave a sardonic smile. Then she flicked the knife towards Storm and cut the rope holding her to the mast.

Mer gripped Storm's shoulder as she slumped forward. She yanked her to her feet and whirled her round, pushing her captive to the side of the ship nearest the Drowned Ones.

Mer put the knife once more to Storm's throat. "You disappoint me, Elder Peggot. I was hoping to join forces with you and attack Bellum Island. I could have offered you all that your people desire: wealth, islands to live on. But it seems I misjudged your intelligence! Storm warned me that the Drowned Ones cannot be trusted. It seems she was right. You just admitted that you intended to kill Waffa once she was no longer useful, merely because she was an Islander. Doubtless you would do the same to me and my people. So it seems I must defeat the Pact myself. It will take a bit longer but a lifetime of hate has taught me patience."

Storm felt Mer's fingers tighten on her shoulder. Her own heart was pounding. The *Narwhal*'s captain was trapped. What would she do?

As if in answer, Mer's voice rang in her ears and the

older girl roared at her crew. "Weigh anchor! Raise the sail!"

Storm heard rushing feet, the clank of winding gear and the grunt of someone hauling on a mainsail rope.

"Dare to double-cross me and you won't live long, Land Grub!" roared Peggot, her face red with rage.

"I intend to keep my end of the bargain," Mer said. Her voice sounded calm, but the hand holding the knife to Storm's throat was shaking. "You can have the witch! She's of no use to me. But this is how it's going to happen. You will row out of arrow shot. Once you have done so, I will put Storm in a canoe and set her adrift."

"Ah, but there is a problem," said Peggot. "I trust you no more than you do me! I think you will keep her for yourself to use as a weapon against the Pact. No, you will give the Weather-witch to us now, Land Grub!" said Peggot. "Or die." She lifted an arm, her fist clenched.

Storm's breath caught in her throat. The Drowned One archers had raised their bows. A dozen arrows were aimed right at her and Mer. From this range the archers could not miss.

"It seems we are at a stalemate," Mer observed over the clanking of winding gear, her voice admirably steady. Storm knew the older girl was playing for time. She needed her ship's sail fully raised or the *Narwhal* had no chance against the pirates' canoes.

"Then I shall break the stalemate!" shouted Peggot. She raised one finger. Storm heard the strumming noise of a bowstring released, and a single arrow flew into the air. Somewhere behind her, a man cried out.

"Ancestors take you!" raged Mer. "You want the Weather-witch? Here you are!"

A sudden shove in the middle of her back, and Storm found herself tumbling over the side of the ship. As she fell, she realised that pushing her overboard was Mer's final, desperate bid to buy enough time to get under sail. Then seawater closed over her head, filled her mouth, flooded her eyes and nose. Storm flailed, trying to swim, but her arms, numb from hours tied to a mast, refused to function. She began to sink.

9

Storm sank slowly, her arms waving vaguely at the dying light from the world of Air. Soon, she knew, she would breathe in the water that would kill her. The thought brought a moment of pure panic. She flailed her arms, tried to kick. And then everything faded.

A thread of music intruded, forced her eyes open. The sun reached long golden fingers underwater, pointing to a dark shape floating beside her. A huge dolphin watched her from an eye the size of a dinner plate.

Live! ordered the music of the sea. *Swim to the light.*

A shaft of sunlight plunged into the watery depths, touching her with warmth. Storm began to move her arms, and this time they pulled her up through the water. Her legs kicked. She had swum before she walked. Now she swam again, weakly and slowly, following the shaft of light until her head broke into air, into wet and splashing and shouting.

She gasped air into her burning lungs, swallowing seawater with it. Through the sea-splash she saw Nim's face loom as he reached out, grabbed her by the wrist and hauled her aboard a canoe. Storm coughed until she retched. As she was vomiting, she heard shouting. She tried to stand, but Nim pushed her flat on to the deck. "Stay down!"

Mer's voice rose above the confusion of sound. The Bellumer was swearing and shouting. Screams, more shouts. Then Nim said, "It's over."

Dreading what she would see, Storm sat up. The Drowned Ones had attacked the *Narwhal*. The male Bellumer lay unmoving on the ship's deck, two arrows protruding from his body. Mer and the female sailor had been taken captive. Mer still struggled with the Drowned Ones holding her, but the older woman stood unresisting, staring in shock at her fallen comrade.

Peggot waited aboard her war canoe, watching her people tie Mer's hands behind her back. Despite the tossing waves, the Elder seemed as sturdy and unmoving as a sea-weathered outcrop of rock, her lined face showing grim satisfaction. Behind her, Storm saw

Rekka. The Fire-witch's fingers twitched and her face glowed with pleasure. Behind her, in the far distance, a plume of black smoke rose – another sea volcano being born. Storm wondered if even this small act of violence had strengthened the Salamander.

The older captive was pulled forward to the very edge of the *Narwhal* to face Peggot. Storm's stomach clenched; Islanders routinely killed Drowned One captives. Would Peggot do the same? But the Elder said, "I am setting you free, Land Grub, but only because I need you to deliver a message: tell your people that their leader is my captive! In a five-day you must send a delegation – no more than three of you – to the westernmost archipelago to the north of Bellum Island. I will be waiting on the largest of those islets.

"There we will negotiate a peace with those of you who rebel against the Pact. Understand this: you will work for us! In return, the Drowned Ones will give you a small portion of Bellum to live on – as our servants. Refuse, and we will kill your headstrong leader. Be assured that we will put her to death if you fail to show up, and more … directly … than she has killed her mother. Upon her death, the rest of you will be left to the mercies of the Pact. Until, that is, we invade and kill you all! Do you understand? Then begone!"

As a furious Mer, hands tied tightly behind her back, was carried, writhing, kicking and shouting threats, on to a war canoe, the last remaining crew member of the *Narwhal* quickly hoisted the mainsail, then ran to the tiller, carefully avoiding the body of her dead companion. The ship slid over the waves and out of sight.

←——————→

Back aboard the Drowned Ones' raft town, Storm watched a furious Mer confront Peggot. "There will be no delegation! My people will never negotiate with you!" raged the tall girl, fists clenched, her long face screwed up in fury. "You've shown that you filthy Drowned One pirates can't be trusted!" All Mer's self-control was broken at last.

Peggot smiled one of her grim smiles. "We all do what we must, Land Grub. And one who betrays her own mother is hardly in a position to talk about trust. Be satisfied: you got your heart's desire – your mother's death is assured. But one must pay for everything in this life and you *will* pay, Land Grub. Make no mistake!"

Peggot cast a glance full of malice at Storm as she said to Nim: "You can have another Land Grub to look after since you seem so fond of them! Keep the Bellum wildcat safe, Nim, or – Earth-witch or no – you will discover the punishment for failure! We have cast all our hopes on this single throw of the bones. I do not intend to lose."

Ignoring Rekka, who had been watching silently, Peggot ordered her sailors to get the raft town underway and strode off, leaping across the ladders connecting the canoes as nimbly as someone half her age.

Nim glared at Mer, who glowered back at him.

"You cannot guard two prisoners, Earth-witch." Rekka stepped forward. Her eyes were red flames. "I will take Storm into my care. I have a plan to help her find her 'lost' magic."

Scoundrel squealed in anger, shaking his fists at the Fire-witch.

"I'll deal with you, at least, creature of the Tortoise!" Rekka's eyes burned scarlet. Her mouth gaped wide, lizard-like. The muscles in her neck moved, and a thin arrow of fire spat towards the monkey. Storm grabbed Scoundrel and tossed him to safety behind her. Then she automatically reached for her magic ... and found nothing.

Nim shoved the witch. "Leave Scoundrel alone!"

Rekka tottered backwards and fell on her bottom with a thump.

The hair on Storm's head seemed to stand straight

up as a sense of danger filled the air like dense smoke. "Don't!" she cried, not sure which of them she was shouting at.

Rekka bounded up, her face shiny with hate. She was panting – deep, noisy hisses. Steam spurted from her nose. Her fingers twitched with the desire to kill.

"If you hurt Nim, the pirates will drown you!" Storm warned.

Rekka snarled and clenched her scarlet talons into fists. But her fear of water seemed to break through her haze of bloodlust. She whirled round to spit into the sea, spewing flame, which hissed as it struck water and disappeared in a cloud of steam.

"I'll not hand Storm over to you, witch," Nim said. His face had grown so pale his freckles glowed. "We need the Weather-witch alive."

"The Salamander will decide her fate, and yours," Rekka retorted. The Fire-witch had recovered her self-control. "And when that day comes, you will regret crossing me, boy. The Tortoise will not be able to save you. No one will save you. Or you!" She threw a simmering glare at Storm, then turned in a whirl of scarlet and strode off.

Storm watched the Salamander's witch until she was out of sight, noticing how, even in her anger, Rekka clung to the hand ropes as she crossed the ladders between the canoes.

All this time, Mer had stood to one side, watching. Now she studied the Drowned One boy like a problem to be solved. "If we had been on dry land, pirate, that witch would have incinerated you. You've certainly made an enemy of her. You're a fool to risk your life for a chattering monkey!"

Scoundrel, who had taken refuge on Nim's shoulders, threw Mer a contemptuous glance and turned to sit with his back to her. Every line of his tiny furry body shouted indignation so loudly that Storm began to laugh. Tears streamed down her eyes, her laughter turned to whoops, and it was only after the others turned to stare at her, including Scoundrel himself – looking highly indignant – that she managed to stop.

"Hysteria," Mer said dismissively.

"I was just comparing his worth to yours!" Storm retorted. "Scoundrel is loyal and kind. Can you say the same?"

Mer shrugged. "You are not even a witch any more, Storm. Your thoughts have as little value as you yourself now."

"Storm is still a witch," Nim said. "And Scoundrel is no ordinary monkey. Rekka was correct – he is an emissary of the Tortoise."

Now it was Mer who crowed with laughter. "Even if the Elementals exist, which I doubt, it says little for the Earth spirit that it would choose a scrawny, verminous weakling like that cling-monkey as its messenger!"

Nim merely shrugged.

"Is it true that you are a witch, pirate boy? An Earth-witch?" Mer seemed to have laid aside her scorn for a moment. She stared at Nim with genuine interest. "You must be powerful to stand up to Rekka like that. But you are far from land. How can you fight when surrounded by water? Surely a pirate Earth-witch is nothing more than a joke! Perhaps that's why Storm finds everything so funny."

"I don't find anything funny in this sorry situation!" Storm retorted. "You have condemned your own mother to a horrible slow death. The Salamander feeds on hatred like yours. Your mother's death will make the Fire Elemental stronger and risk—"

"The Balance, I know." Mer laughed contemptuously. "Stories to scare little children. The only balance I recognise is that of power. As for my mother, Waffa has earned this death!"

"And are you happy?" Nim asked her. "What will you do, Land Grub, now that you no longer have your hate to live for?"

Mer scowled at him. "Survive!" she growled. "To pay you and your Elders back for your treachery!"

"Of course. Someone new to hate." Nim shrugged. "Unfortunately, it's my job to make sure you don't get yourself killed through sheer spite." He gestured towards the middle of the raft town. "We go that way. I will show you where you'll be living while you are our … guest."

←——————→

The Drowned Ones' raft town slipped through the waves of the Inner Sea like a manta ray, scout canoes making sure the town easily avoided the ships travelling the trading routes. Now Storm understood how the pirates stalked their prey, but Peggot was not hunting, she was hiding while she waited out the five-day.

Storm and Mer were locked in a small cabin somewhere at the heart of the raft town maze. Over the rest of the day, Mer grew less angry and more thoughtful. But the Bellumer did not confide in Storm. She spoke to her fellow prisoner only when absolutely necessary, and then with hardly disguised contempt.

Storm barely noticed. She could not stop thinking about Waffa drifting helplessly with a few days' worth of water and no shelter from the merciless sun. She had no fondness for the woman, but it was a horrible, lingering death.

That night, after a meagre dinner of fish and dried seaweed cakes, the nightmare that had haunted her childhood returned. In her dream, Da was tossed on the waves, clutching a wooden plank of his boat. He drifted beneath a raging sun until, as she watched, helpless even to cry out to him, her father's fingers let go at last, and he sank beneath the waves.

Something prodding her in the side woke her from her dream. Her heart was pounding, her face wet with tears. A grumpy Mer, lying next to her on the seaweed stuffed sack that served as mattress for them both, was complaining loudly: "Shut up, Storm! I'm trying to sleep and your whining is enough to give me bad dreams too."

"Sorry," muttered Storm.

"You kept shouting about not being able to save someone. Save who?" The older girl paused. "You were crying. You sounded … desperate."

"My father. I told you, remember? But of course you don't remember: you never think about anything that isn't about you!"

Mer did not reply. Storm snorted, then shifted on the rustling mattress, releasing the seaweed perfume of salt and dead fish. Just as she was drifting off, Mer spoke into the darkness of the windowless hut, her voice unusually quiet.

"When I first met you, Storm, you surprised me. You weren't like anyone else. You didn't care about status or wealth. I began to imagine what it would be like to have you as a friend. I wanted to be more like you – to be happy in my own skin. To be kind. I know I'm not a good person. Life isn't that simple. But I keep wishing…" There was a sigh, almost a sob. Then: "*What is wrong with me?*"

Storm kept her breathing slow, pretending to be asleep. Mer hadn't meant her to hear her confession – especially that last whispered cry of anguish. As for her, she wished she could unhear it! It made dealing with Mer more complicated, and she had enough to worry about. Storm lay in the dark listening to Mer toss and turn until at last the older girl's breathing slowed and she slept.

Perhaps, somehow, she could find a way to get through to Mer… Storm lay quietly in the night-dark for a long time, listening to Mer breathing and thinking. It seemed she hadn't given up on defeating the Salamander after all. The realisation kept her awake long into the night.

IO

The second day after Mer's capture dawned all too soon. Storm felt like she had only just got to sleep when the door to their prison opened. She peered bleary-eyed up at someone in the doorway, transformed into a dark silhouette by the bright morning sunshine.

"Breakfast," Nim announced.

Mer was already up, sitting as far from Storm as possible. She silently followed Nim out into the sunshine.

Hunger helped to wake Storm. She used the privy bucket then took it outside to dump the contents over the side of the canoe. She rinsed the bucket in the sea and replaced it in the hut. Mer watched, making no offer to help. *She's probably never emptied a privy bucket in her life*, said her mind-voice. Storm shrugged. She wouldn't trade her past for Mer's lifetime of luxury on Bellum. She'd had Dain for a mother and all the chores in the world were worth that.

Nim ate his breakfast with them. Storm joined the other two where they sat beside the steaming iron pot of dried squid and seaweed stew, taking turns to refill the coconut shells that served as bowls. Storm was so hungry that the watery stew tasted delicious.

"What will your people decide?" Nim asked the older girl, when the iron pot had been scraped empty. "Will they agree to Peggot's terms?"

Mer's eyes narrowed. "No. Every Islander knows we can't trust you pirate scum. Look how you treated me! My people aren't that stupid. Your Elder will find she can't invade Bellum without our help. She'll have to let me go in the end."

"You don't know Peggot," Nim said shortly. "What of the witches? What of Linnet, the old Earth-witch? Do you have news of him?"

"Why should I tell you anything?" Mer stared at him, her upper lip curled with the unconscious arrogance of the Pact. "You're a peasant. And a Drowned One to boot."

"And you, Land Grub, are my prisoner." Nim said smugly, and grinned at Mer's sudden scowl. "Not liking that, are you?"

"You are so selfish, Mer!" Storm burst in, her anger getting the better of her. "Don't you understand that every time a human kills another it feeds the Salamander? Every act of hatred, of revenge, of war – it all makes Fire stronger. By sending your mother to her death you give power to the Element that hates life. Do you *want* a world of fire and barren stone?"

Mer stared, open-mouthed, and Storm felt herself flushing with embarrassment. She hadn't meant to say any of that. There was no point: Mer would never listen. The Bellumer had proved that she stubbornly insisted on believing what best suited the story she had made about her life.

Mer recovered and, typically, attacked: "Don't bring my mother into this! I hope she's dead by now!"

"I thought you wanted her to suffer," said Storm. "Why else insist she take three days' worth of water?"

Mer shrugged and turned to Nim. "You don't believe this nonsense she's spouting, do you?"

"I believe what the Tortoise tells me," Nim said evenly. "And the evidence of my own eyes. New volcanoes are exploding out of the Sea of Drowned Islands, where my long-ago ancestors' homes sank in the ancient war between Fire and Water. I've seen new clouds of ash, fountains of lava. The fish are fleeing south as the Sea of Drowned Islands grows ever hotter. Storm is right: the Salamander feeds on our hate. It grows stronger every day. War between the Elementals is close."

"Closer than you can imagine, Tortoise boy!" Rekka hitched herself carefully on to their canoe, gripping the rope ladder.

Her progress was so slow and fearful that Storm bit back a laugh. Rekka liked to make an entrance, but this probably wasn't what she had in mind.

All desire to laugh faded when, safely past open water, the Fire-witch pointed a long scarlet claw at Storm. "She's coming with me! Your Elders have given me permission to question her. You can escort her to my cabin."

"No!"

Storm could have bitten her tongue for crying out in fear and shaming herself. She felt her face grow hot. She wouldn't show fear again to the Fire-witch. She clenched her fists and waited for whatever happened next.

Nim jumped to his feet. "Storm isn't going anywhere with you. Not until I check this out."

"No need, Tortoise boy. I have your Elder's seal here." Rekka showed her white teeth in a sharky grin.

She held out a carved wooden tablet.

Nim took the seal in his hand and frowned down at it. Storm could see that he was defeated. Nim could refuse Rekka, but not Peggot.

Her glance darted to the Fire-witch and she met flame-haunted eyes staring right back at her. What did Rekka intend to do with her? Storm swallowed a dry lump in her throat and wished she had not eaten so much soup.

←——————→

"You might as well stop looking at the door. He's not going to rescue you this time. Besides…" Rekka put her hands behind her head and grinned. As soon as they had entered her hut, the witch had thrown herself on to the pile of mats that Storm realised must be her bed.

The place stank of stale sweat and fish oil. An under-tunic lay crumpled on the floor and a pair of sandals lay where Rekka had kicked them off. A pile of gnawed fish bones cluttered the small table. Dust motes danced in the sunlight pouring in at the small window. Storm had never been in such a dirty, disorganised room. She was shocked for a moment, until she remembered that Rekka had raised herself from early childhood. She had never had a chance to learn how things were done.

Feral, said her mind-voice. *Like a half-tamed civet. Even more dangerous because you can't trust them to even know what is normal.*

"Don't look so frightened, Storm," said the Fire-witch. "You and I have much to discuss. Things are about to look up for you." Rekka smiled at her and Storm's mouth went dry.

The Fire-witch looked happier than Storm had ever seen her. She smiled broadly at Storm. A long red tongue flicked out from between her teeth, like a lizard scenting the air. "I want to make a confession," she said. "Do you mind?"

"Does it matter if I do?"

"No. How clever of you to know that, child." Rekka was enjoying herself. Confidence rolled off her in waves, like the oily smell of her body. Storm guessed that the Fire-witch feared and hated water so much she never washed.

"The truth is, I'm fond of you, Storm. Now, now, don't look so shocked. You must have guessed my feelings. Why else would you still be alive? Yes, I find I'm very fond of you. For one thing, you are … you *were* a worthy opponent. I have never faced a witch nearly as powerful as myself. It was all just a bit too easy before we met." Rekka tilted her head, waiting for Storm's reply.

Storm bowed her head stiffly. "I am pleased if my efforts provided you with some small entertainment." What diabolical plan was Rekka up to?

"So polite," sighed Rekka. "So well brought up. I understand that you were close to your mother."

Storm frowned. She was not going to discuss Dain with the Salamander's creature!

"I hated mine," said the Fire-witch. "In fact, I still hate her. She lives still on the nasty little island where I was born. She and my father, and all the others that tried to kill me." Rekka had stopped smiling. "They live, but not for much longer…"

"What do you mean?"

"Don't pretend to be a fool – I hate false modesty! You know perfectly well that I intend to destroy them. You have the imagination to realise that their destruction has been my intention from the moment they left me to die on that frozen rock. I survived that place – survived more than you can ever imagine – for only one reason: to watch them die!"

Storm shuddered at the blast of hatred that hit her.

"Yes," Rekka said with a chuckling laugh, "your friend Mer and I have much in common. Only I intend to kill *both* my parents, plus every single living soul on my birth island! But even you cannot guess why I have waited so many years – a lifetime. I could have taken my revenge at any time these past thirty years. Why didn't I? Come. You're a clever girl. Tell me why I've waited until now!" The witch's eyes flared wide and she stared at Storm expectantly.

A chill like a serpent's breath crept up Storm's spine. She couldn't tear her eyes away from Rekka's face, from the dancing fire in the pupils of her eyes. Rekka was right: Storm knew the answer. It had to be, and it was too horrible!

"I think you have waited for your revenge at the Salamander's order. It made you wait until the time was right. Now Fire makes its move against the other Elementals. It thinks it is nearly strong enough to win, so allows you to take your revenge. When you kill everyone on your birth island, the Salamander believes that hideous act of hate will finally give it the power it needs to beat the Dolphin and destroy the Balance!"

"Ahhhhh." Rekka's sigh was long and blissful. "Well done, Storm. Indeed, we have already begun. When Mer's mother dies, the final moments will have started. Murder of one's parents is so powerful, you see. Such hate is especially nourishing to the Salamander.

"Then, when I kill not just my parents, but every

living thing on the island that begat me, Fire will rise to new heights of power! That alone may be enough. If it isn't, war between the Drowned Ones and Islanders is now inevitable. And that must make the Salamander invulnerable! The Dolphin, Tortoise and Albatross will know the bitterness of defeat. The Salamander will crush them and take the world for itself!"

"But…" Rekka, like Mer, seemed to be so obsessed with revenge that she was blinded by her hatred. "If that happens, you won't live to enjoy your revenge. We will all die. All life will die!"

The Fire-witch opened her mouth wide. Storm flinched. But instead of fire, Rekka spewed laughter. "You are desperate, poor child. Or deluded. Is that what the Elementals tell you? Lies! Why would the Salamander kill all human life? It needs us to worship its beauty and strength. Those Chosen by Fire will be allowed to live. True, the world will be changed forever. There will be little water and that tamed to still ponds. The seas will cease to exist. But think of all the lovely hot, dry land for us to live on then. Who cares about a few fish?"

"And those not Chosen by Fire?"

"They will die, yes. Why not? The world will be cleansed of all the acolytes of puny Earth, Water and

Air. Then, once their Chosen humans are no more, the lesser Elementals will become weak and will be kept in thrall to Fire forever!"

Hopelessness washed over Storm's soul like a brown haze. Rekka refused to see the truth. Hopelessness washed over ... refused to see the truth. Storm tried one last time: "The Salamander lies! You will die along with every living creature. You mean nothing to it – you're a tool to be used and discarded."

The witch surged to her feet, reached down a clawed hand and grabbed her prisoner by the front of her tunic. Rekka lifted Storm with horrific strength and shook her until Storm's teeth chattered against each other so hard she thought they would break. The Fire-witch tossed her away, and Storm collapsed on the wooden floor of the hut, gasping to get her breath.

"Fool! And I was going to offer you so much!"

Tiny and fearful, Storm's mind-voice spoke: *Pretend. Play along.*

"Offer me? What could you have to offer me?" Storm hated hearing the fear in her voice, but it seemed that at last she had said the right thing. Rage melted from Rekka's face and was replaced with cunning.

"Not *me*, Storm. I offer nothing. It is the Salamander who offers everything!"

Storm frowned. Whatever she had expected, it hadn't been this. The Fire Elemental had tried to kill her too many times to count. "What do you mean?"

"Have you forgotten? You are one of the most fortunate of humans! You, like me, are a Child of the Salamander!"

11

It was a lie! The Salamander had tried to kill her on her Choosing Day.

Rekka grinned. She was enjoying this. "Did the Salamander speak to you on the day of your Choosing?"

"Not the way you mean—"

"Did you hear the voice of the Salamander. Yes or no?"

"It doesn't mean anything!" Her stomach churned. Storm had tried to forget that long-ago day when she had stood in the middle of the Salamander's shrine on her home island of Yanlin, nearly dead from breathing in choking smoke and ash, and heard a slithering voice ordering her to give up and die.

"It spoke only to threaten, to break my will. It tried to kill me!"

"Of course." Rekka shrugged. "You were a threat. Eliminating you was the only sensible course of action then. But –" she shrugged again – "you have a talent for surviving. And your potential for magic is strong, very strong. The Salamander has decided you can be of greater use to it alive."

"But I *have* no magic."

"Ah." And now Rekka not only smiled, she beamed. "Join us, Storm. Join us, and you *will*!"

Storm suppressed a shudder.

Play along! urged her mind-voice. *Pretend. Play for time.*

"The … Salamander would give me magic?"

"More than you can imagine. What are Air and Water compared to Fire? Weak, insignificant powers—"

"That nearly killed you when we last met."

Rekka shrugged. "'Nearly' is useless. But I admit you were a worthy opponent. Just think, Storm, what you and I could do together. Think of your power when you have Fire at your command! Besides, the Albatross and Dolphin have scorned you, abandoned you to your fate as my parents abandoned me. You owe them nothing!"

Storm held her breath and waited, nerves tingling, mind confused. Was Rekka telling the truth, or was it all just another trick? Did the Salamander really want her as its agent? Was the Elemental offering to make her a Fire-witch? For a heartbeat she imagined walking unhurt through flames and drinking liquid fire, only to spew it forth like a mythical dragon god.

"Think of it, Storm!" hissed Rekka. "Join us, and you will be the most powerful witch the world has ever known!" She reached forward; her hand grasped Storm's. Her skin was dry and smooth, her grip warm. It was a shock. Storm had expected her to feel scaly and cold-blooded.

The witch leaned close. The red pupils of her eyes danced with light. Storm could not look away.

Rekka's voice twined through her thoughts. "We connect, you and I. Sisters in Fire. You feel it, as much as I. You are special, unique. Join us and you will be cherished as you deserve! Reborn as Storm of the Salamander's Fury! We will fight together, you and I. We will overcome all opposition. We will be the champions of a new world! The Salamander will never abandon you, like the Albatross, like the Tortoise. They never loved you as Fire does!"

Rekka leaned even closer. "Feel the warmth of the Salamander's love!" Hot and spicy, the witch's breath flowed into Storm's face. Before she could stop herself, Storm had breathed it in. Her lungs grew hot. Her whole body seemed to glow with a strength she had never before known. She had never felt this alive! *What was going on? Had Teanu been wrong? Was she really a true Child of Fire? Rekka's words made sense. Why would the Salamander destroy all life? It merely wanted to be worshipped, like all the Elementals.*

The Tortoise has never asked you to worship it! chided her mind-voice. *Neither has the Dolphin or Albatross. She is lying! She must be…*

"The Albatross and Tortoise betrayed you!" Rekka cried, her face nearly touching Storm's, red eyes burning. "They left you to die! The Dolphin cares for no human: did it not kill your father? Only the Salamander can be trusted to protect you! Fire will give you such power that no one can ever hurt you again. You will be invulnerable! Fire will never betray you as Water has, as Air has. Become one of us. Join me!"

The witch laid her hands on Storm's shoulders, and she felt a shock through her entire body. Her mouth dried; every strand of her hair seemed to stand on end and writhe like a snake. Her blood burned; her heart pounded. Was this what power felt like? Was this new Storm who she was meant to become?

Rekka said, "I will never abandon you, as your mother did!"

The spell broke.

Storm shuddered with revulsion. "That is your story, Rekka, not mine! My mother didn't abandon me. She died fighting for the people and island she loved. You have never loved. I almost feel sorry for you!" Storm pushed the witch away, unable to bear any longer the touch of long grasping fingers, the hot breath in her face.

Rekka, taken by surprise, sprawled backwards. The Fire-witch growled and leapt to her feet.

Storm backed away, but there was no place to run. Rekka's fingers twitched wildly. Storm recognised the signs. She was about to be incinerated, and there was nothing she could do about it except to die bravely, as Dain had done.

The Fire-witch snarled, white teeth gleaming. "You are lucky, brat, that I cannot burn you to melted flesh and charred bone, as you deserve!" She closed her twitching fingers into bony fists. "Not yet. Not while only a few wooden boards stand between me and foul Water. But wait, only wait…"

Storm let go of the breath she had been holding. Thank the seas! Her fear of water meant that Rekka would not kill her where she stood. But the danger was far from over. The witch began to pace back and forth in the small room, growling and swearing. Her eyes blazed. At last, when she had calmed herself sufficiently, the Fire-witch turned to face Storm again.

"You are a fool!" Rekka spat the words. "The Salamander offered you life. My master offered power beyond your puny imagination. You will regret spurning us! We will not forget, Storm of Yanlin. We will kill you. Be certain. It is only a question of time."

The smouldering hate in the Fire-witch's eyes was as hot as a bonfire. Storm flinched backwards, her left hand automatically covering the scar on her right wrist where the Salamander had once grabbed her with a hand of flame.

"You're right," Storm found it hard to speak: her mouth tasted scorched. "All will be decided in time. And the S-salamander will lose!"

Rekka laughed, her mood changing once more with lightning speed. "Ah Storm, you don't believe that. You can't even make such a ridiculous claim without your tongue stumbling over the stupidity of your words. But you are brave, and I like that. It won't save you, of course. When the time comes for me to kill you, remember what could have been. I will miss you, I think." She shrugged, but not before Storm caught a glimpse of something that astounded her.

Loneliness? No, she must have been mistaken. And she could barely see at all now. Her eyes were aching, streaming. They felt sunburned. What had Rekka done to her?

"A sad waste of potential," the Fire-witch continued. "But you made your choice. Now you will learn that no one refuses the Salamander and survives! You will die in agony. Sooner than you might think, dear Storm!" With that, Rekka turned and marched out of the hut. Before Storm could calm down enough to think through what had just happened, she returned, two Drowned One soldiers in her wake. "Take the girl back to your Earth-witch!"

Storm felt the heat of glittering eyes boring into her back long after she had left the hut. The feeling continued throughout the journey back to Nim and Mer, long after her enemy could still be watching her. Only when she was pushed into Nim's hut and Scoundrel jumped into her arms with a cry of happiness did Storm let herself believe she really had survived her latest meeting with Rekka the Fire-witch.

Nim and Mer seemed to be in the middle of a conversation. The Bellum rebel frowned as Storm entered the room. Mer stalked away to sit in a corner, ignoring them both as Nim began to question Storm about her interrogation.

←——————→

The sun had barely passed the midday mark when more soldiers arrived at Nim's hut. "The Islander witch is to come with us. Peggot wants her." The soldier flashed the Elder's token, but Nim didn't even bother to check it this time.

"Why?" His voice was so fierce Storm's heart sank. Whatever was about to happen, it wasn't good.

The solider hesitated, then said, "The town has set sail for the reef."

Nim went very still.

"What does this mean?" Storm demanded. "What happens at this reef?" She saw the Drowned One boy exchange a look with Mer.

What are these two up to? asked her mind-voice. *They're keeping things from you. You're on your own and you need to stop hoping either of them will help you!*

"I'm coming," Nim told the guard, ignoring Storm's question. He refused to look at her. "Which means she has to come." Nim pointed at Mer.

"She'll have to be tied then," said the female soldier.

"Don't you dare!" Mer began. But Nim nodded and the guard took a length of rope from the wall and tied Mer's hands behind her back with efficient ruthlessness.

"And her?" The guard nodded at Storm.

"That won't be necessary." Nim finally met Storm's gaze.

Storm raised her chin. Scoundrel whimpered and leapt on to her shoulders, clinging tightly to her neck. "I'm ready," she said.

It was a lie. Whatever was about to happen, she didn't think she was going to enjoy it. She wondered if she would even survive it.

12

The wind had picked up. The raft town of the Drowned Ones sped over the waves, lurching to the top of each watery cliff before dropping down with stomach-emptying suddenness and crashing into the next valley, shooting spray everywhere.

The wind cooled the sun's fierceness. Spray drenched Storm from head to toe, but her clothes dried almost at once in the midday heat. She was watching Nim argue with his Elders.

The old people stood in a half-circle, facing their Earth-witch. Mer was tethered like a goat to one of the gate poles of the Elder's cabin. Near her, devouring Storm with unblinking scarlet eyes, was Rekka the Fire-witch, motionless except for her fingers.

"Why are you doing this?" Nim shouted. "You know

the Fire-witch can't be trusted, and we need Storm alive!" Nim and Peggot squared off, toe to toe. They looked like wrestlers about to start battle, neither prepared to give ground. One look at Peggot's face had told Storm Nim's arguments would be useless. But he was a stubborn as her cousin Minnow.

"Do not overstep yourself, Earth-witch!" warned Peggot. "You still answer to your Elders. The decision is ours! The Fire-witch reports that her interrogation of the Weather-witch was a failure. The girl still insists she has no magic. I intend to see if that is true. And we only need one of them, Nim. Your magic, and that of the Fire-witch, will be enough to defeat the Pact. Bellum Island will be ours!"

"Bellum is only one island!" shouted Nim. "Enough for a few raft towns, two or three. Most of our people would still be homeless. You agreed to my plan. I need the Weather-witch! I will build us new islands! Dozens! And Storm will help me turn them into gardens of plenty, sheltered from the worst storms. We will grow enough food to feed all our tribe!"

"That dream of yours will take years, boy! I don't even know if you are powerful enough to do what you hope – to pull the earth up through the sea with magic and build new islands. It may merely be a boy's fantasy.

Even if your Earth magic *is* strong enough, many of us would not live to see your project completed. And Bellum is rich and fertile. It exists now."

"Do you forget that Fire is already eating the seas? You have seen the new volcanoes sprouting, witnessed shoals of fish fleeing the Sea of Drowned Islands. I told you of the Salamander's plans. Do you doubt the Tortoise? I urged you to kill the Salamander's witch! Instead, you let her trick you into a contest that may destroy the one person who can save us all! I won't let you do this, Peggot!"

"Do you dare rebel against your Elders and your tribe?" Peggot's sturdy, square body seemed to swell. "There will be no lingering war for the Salamander to feed off. We take Bellum and that is all. Time to worry about the Balance when that is done."

Nim made an impatient gesture.

"I have decided!" Peggot roared. "You will obey. Or do you choose to throw your life away?"

The other Elders began to mutter darkly. The Drowned One warriors tightened their grips on swords and bows. And all watched Nim. He stood, breathing hard, sweat beading on face and shoulders.

He looks as if he has run a long and hard path, thought Storm, *only to arrive too late*. Things were seeming less and less real to her. It was as if she watched from far away. Nim stepped back and bent his head in defeat. When he turned to look at her, she was able to meet his gaze calmly. It was up to fate to decide what happened now – fate, and the Elemental spirits.

Peggot nodded, satisfied that Nim's rebellion was at an end. "Perhaps the Weather-witch will win," she told him. "And we will know, one way or another, whether the Elementals have really taken away her magic, for if they have, she will die."

"Storm will die whether she has magic or not!" Rekka smiled at her rival. "We are to duel again, child." She spoke as if they were alone. "And this time, I will win. I warned you. You had your chance. Do not expect mercy."

"I do not." Storm's heart began to pound as she thought of the coming duel between her and the Fire-witch. Only it would not be a duel – just the spectacle of a predator chasing down its prey.

←——————→

The raft town sped over the waves towards a circle of sea-lashed stone. It was a caldera: a dead volcano. The remains of the volcano's mouth had become a reef guarding a chunky circle of rock – a small island with a miniature bay and a minute crescent of shingled beach.

Peggot roared an order to drop anchor. Section by section, the raft town slowed as dozens of anchor ropes tightened. Soon the town was safely anchored in the choppy water facing a narrow gap in the reef. Beyond lay the tiny bay with its scrap of beach. Peggot turned to Storm.

"You and the Fire-witch will be landed on the island. We call it The Judgement Isle. When our people have disagreements that cannot be solved any other way, the parties are brought here. Death makes the final judgement. Do you still claim to have lost your magic, girl?"

"I have no magic," Storm said simply.

Peggot studied her. "You believe it. Well, then you will die. And it will be a bad death, Storm of Yanlin. I will not mourn you. You owe me a death. When the Fire-witch kills you, my brother's spirit will be avenged at last and able to find peace in the land of the Ancestors."

Storm returned Peggot's gaze unflinchingly. "And if Nim is right? Will you aid Rekka and the Salamander in destroying the world?"

"I will see her dead first, girl. Don't worry about that!"

Storm, glancing at the Fire-witch, thought the Elder

100

might have benefited from the sight of Rekka's face just at that moment. A chill shivered down her spine.

"Enough talk!" barked Peggot. She turned to Nim, her scowl ferocious. "You, Earth-witch, will stay on board this raft and do nothing to interfere. If you try to help the Weather-witch, you will be dead to us. Exiled. You will be cast out and hunted to the end of your days. Do I make myself clear?"

Nim's face had gone pale. He nodded tersely. His eyes darted to Storm, then away. He looked hunted. She understood. Really she did – there was nothing he nor anyone else could do now to save her. But the defeat in Nim's eyes made her more scared than she had ever been in her life.

"You!" Peggot pointed at a Drowned One warrior. "Stay with Nim. Keep an eye on him and the Bellum girl." Confident that her witch had given in, Peggot reached out and gripped Nim's hand. "Trust me, boy. All will be well. Perhaps, in time, we shall even build some of your islands. But we shall take some from the Islanders first! With the Fire-witch's help. You and she together will make us unstoppable."

Nim looked Peggot square in the eyes. "I am a Drowned One. I will work for my people with all my heart and every drop of my sweat and blood!"

Peggot smiled, nodded, stepped back. "I knew I could trust you. You are our Earth-witch – the first our tribe has had for generations. You have been sent by the Tortoise to help us win the fight against the Islander scum, to win us land of our own to live on, to grow food on. No Drowned One would ever betray their people for the likes of an Islander girl!"

But Peggot did not reverse her orders to the warrior, who took up a position with his back to the cabin, watching both Nim and Mer. The Elder indicated with a jerk of her head that Storm was to move off. "That way, witch."

"Go to Nim, Scoundrel!" Storm tried to unwrap the animal's long arms from round her neck. But the cling-monkey lived up to his name and held on tighter than ever. Oddly enough, he made no sound – no scolding or whimpering. "Nim, help me get him off!"

The Drowned One boy shook his head. "Let him go with you. He'll come to no harm. Scoundrel is the only friend you will have with you when the time comes."

Something in Nim's voice caught her attention. He had put an emphasis "… *when the time comes*". She searched his face eagerly, but his expression gave nothing away. Perhaps it had only been her imagination, but even so, Storm felt the faintest stirring of hope. She nodded farewell to the Drowned One boy, and hoped he understood that, whatever happened, she had no hard feelings. Then Storm turned away and walked to the waiting canoe.

13

The wind screamed. Storm's hair and tunic flapped wildly as she jumped into the surf and battled through the frantic water to the beach. Scoundrel chittered in her ear, and she patted him awkwardly.

She turned to see Rekka being carried on the back of a huge Drowned One warrior wading through the surf. Wind and spray battered the Fire-witch, her scarlet tunic flapping damply. She was screeching, hitting the man with her fist to hurry him along, her terror of water plain on her face.

"Yes," Storm said to the cling-monkey as Scoundrel became more agitated. "I know she's frightened of water, but I don't have Water magic any more. She's stronger than me so I couldn't hold her under the water long enough to drown her. Besides, she would

incinerate me before I got close enough to grab her."
But even as she spoke, her mind was working, trying
to find a plan to defeat death. Could she simply jump
into the sea and swim out of the reach of Rekka's fire?
Maybe, except that the Drowned Ones would stop her,
scoop her out of the water and send her right back to
face Rekka. No, there was no escape by sea.

There must be a way! insisted her mind-voice.

If I could knock her out somehow, mused Storm.
Throw a rock? There were plenty on the beach, but
they were tiny. Her eyes searched frantically for a large
enough stone.

Rekka jumped from the tall warrior's back as soon as
he touched dry land. She lunged up the shingle towards
drier footing where she stood, panting and shivering
and shaking spray from her tunic, water-darkened until
it looked black in the sun's glare. The canoe carrying
Peggot landed next. The Elder was over the side at
once, marching easily through the surge up on to the
beach. She advanced until she stood at a halfway point
on the beach between Storm and Rekka.

"Combatants!" Peggot called, shouting over the roar
of the wind. "You are charged to fight to the death. The
battle is to commence once we have all taken our places
in the viewing area." She pointed to the surrounding

ring of volcanic rock, the rim of the caldera.

Dozens of figures had already landed on the ridge from the raft town and were now climbing to the top of the ridge. The Drowned One audience would have a view that circled the entire islet. The perfect spot from which to watch Rekka hunt her down.

"The signal to commence battle will be the raising of my banner on the central ridge. At that point there are no rules, merely a fight to the death using whatever weapons you can find. And magic, of course. " She pointed to a spot on the central ridge. "That is where we will hoist the flag. You must not attack before then, or the battle will be stopped and the culprit tied to an anchor, rowed out to deep water and pushed into the sea!" Peggot looked directly at Rekka as she said this, and the Fire-witch smiled.

"Don't worry, Old Drowned One," said Rekka. "I don't need to cheat to win. The Salamander is with me!" Her fingers twitched, and she turned to stare at Storm. Even from this distance, Storm could see flame glowing in the pupils of the witch's eyes. Steam began to rise from the Fire-witch's clothes, drying the dark colour of her tunic to bright scarlet in the blink of an eye.

Fear twisted Storm's stomach into a painful knot. Her

heart thudded. Then she yelped in pain as Scoundrel reached up and pinched her earlobe with sharp-nailed fingers. She looked where the monkey was pointing and noticed, for the first time, a series of what looked like a ring of tidal pools behind the knoll where they stood. *Are they deep enough to shelter in?* asked her mind-voice.

Even if the pools were deep enough to submerge her whole body in, Rekka would boil the water dry in a matter of heartbeats. Still, there were lots of the pools scattered over that side of the islet. Maybe if she dodged from pool to pool, she could at least buy time to find some throwing stones.

Scoundrel suddenly hugged her tightly, then leapt down from her shoulder and scrambled, long-armed and tail swinging furiously, over the shingle and out of sight to another small hillock behind the pools.

It's for the best, her mind-voice said. But Storm suddenly felt even more vulnerable, which was stupid because a small monkey could not protect her from Rekka.

Peggot and her entourage were marching back to their canoes. Storm watched the Drowned Ones launch into the bay. A few strokes of the paddle and they were at the base of the surrounding reef. She glanced at Rekka. Would fear of the Drowned Ones stop her from cheating?

The Fire-witch stood a mere arrow's flight from Storm. Howls of wind roared through the gap in the reef, straight on to the shingled beach. The witch's scarlet tunic flapped wildly and Rekka's long black plaits snaked behind her, writhing as if they were alive. Seagulls screamed as they passed overhead, blown sideways on the strengthening wind. The Fire-witch met her gaze, watching her with a look that made the hair on the back of Storm's neck lift.

Something made Storm dodge to one side as she turned to look at the reef. On its highest point she saw a yellow flag rise up a wooden post. It was the signal to start fighting!

Fire lashed the shingle where Storm had been standing a heartbeat before. But she was already leaping away, scrambling desperately over the shingle, feet sliding, falling to her knees. Flame erupted right in front of her, scorching the place she would have reached had she not fallen. And then she scrabbled up and was running again.

14

As Storm plunged headlong into the first of the rock pools, she heard the Fire-witch gloat: "Do you think that puddle will stop me?" Even as her ears filled with water and she slithered like an eel, seeking the depths of the pool, she heard Rekka's laughter. Mad. Triumphant.

She waited as long as she dared, then rolled out of the pool. She was up and sprinting away towards the next, the wind screaming in her ears. Behind her came a loud hiss like a dragon's belch. A heat-wall of steam hit Storm from behind, nearly knocking her down. She looked over her shoulder and saw steam explode into the sky like smoke. The pool she had sheltered in had boiled away to nothing. The Fire-witch met her eyes, showed pointed teeth in a feral grin and began the chase, hitching up her scarlet tunic as her long legs ate up the distance between them.

Storm saw a fist-sized rock and raced to scoop it up, but a bolt of fire struck the ground in front of her before she could reach it. There was a stink of scorched seaweed and a hiss of steam. The damp shingle dried in an instant. Storm dodged left, and ran for the next pool. She felt a searing sting in the arm that had reached out for the rock. The shock of cold water washed away the pain for the two heartbeats she allowed herself to hide beneath the water. And then she was out and off again. Another blast of steam as Rekka boiled away the pond she had just left. One less hiding place.

The ground here was gravel or giant boulders. She had to outrun and dodge the Fire-witch long enough to find some throwing rocks. The water pools would soon be blasted to steam and there was no other shelter.

Fire struck just ahead of her. Storm grunted as she jumped back, fell, stumbled up. Behind her, she heard a laugh and realised that Rekka was playing with her. When she had had enough fun, the Fire-witch would stop missing.

Somewhere ahead of her, the cry of a cling-monkey rang out. Storm jumped sideways just as a rope of fire lashed at her. Stumbling to stay on her feet, she ignored a burning sensation on her left ear and the stink of singed hair, listening instead for Scoundrel's screams. Then, through the smoke and steam boiling up from the ground, Storm saw a small orange-furred animal hurtling towards the Fire-witch. Faster than thought, the monkey dashed up to the Fire-witch, bit her on the calf of her right leg and raced on.

"No!" Storm shouted.

The witch screamed, her shriek drowning out the howl of the wind. Blood the exact colour of her tunic streamed down her leg. Scoundrel had bitten deeply. The witch whirled round to give chase and nearly fell. Cursing and limping, she followed the monkey.

"Run, Scoundrel! Go!" Storm raced after the Fire-witch. At last she spotted a perfect throwing stone and scooped it up as she ran. Scoundrel was risking his life to distract her enemy. It was time to attack!

Rekka limped in pursuit of the cling-monkey, tossing handfuls of fire one after another, arms swinging like a windmill. The missiles exploded in steam and sparks, landing closer and closer to the monkey.

The cling-monkey reached the top of a small rise of land too low to be called a hill and turned to face the Fire-witch. He stood still and silent as a sentinel as the Salamander's witch limped ever nearer. Storm sprinted, but she was too far away for a decent throw.

She wasn't going to get there in time! A sudden gust of wind barrelled into her, spraying mist into her eyes, nearly knocking her off her feet.

Rekka cackled in joy and anticipation. "I wasn't going to forget about you, messenger of the Tortoise. Never fear. But you make it easy for me. And yes, I'd rather deal with you first and save Storm for last. Mind, you're hardly worth the energy it takes to roast you, you flea-bitten little—"

Spewing spittle from between bared teeth, the Fire-witch raised her right arm, scarlet-spiked fingers pointing and twitching.

"Leave him!" Storm threw her stone with all her strength and skill – but it wasn't enough: the stone would not reach.

At the sight, Rekka roared with laughter and turned her back in contempt. Theatrically, she raised her hands once more.

Storm's stone hit the ground and bounced. It kept on going, bouncing and rolling towards the Fire-witch, gathering shingle as it went, picking up gravel and fine stones as it travelled until a tumbling, bouncing mass of earth, stone and mud rolled straight for the Fire-witch.

This was magic! Storm slid to a stop. Someone was

singing! The song told of rich mud and layered rock, of black silt and the richness of green life. It told of seeds sprouting, bees humming, birdsong, the green smell of young rice. It was the song of the Tortoise! It must be, though she had never heard it before.

As fire leapt from the tips of Rekka's twitching fingers and hurtled towards Scoundrel, the ground directly in front of the monkey rose like a living thing. A wall of stone, gravel and mud swelled head high. The fire-bolt struck it and was dashed to harmless sparks. Then Storm's rolling ball of shingle thudded into Rekka from behind, knocking her to her knees and splattering her with sand and stone.

A shriek of sheer rage and frustration rose from the islet and echoed around the reef. The Salamander's witch scrambled to her feet. She screamed in fury and blasted the earth wall sheltering her prey. But as she drew breath for her next attack, the wall thickened, widened. Her third fire-bolt met the fate of the first two.

"You foul, treacherous little liar!" A snarling Rekka whirled round to face Storm. "You haven't lost your magic at all! And you're an Earth-witch as well. Well, none of it will save you!"

The Fire-witch seemed to swell. She flung her head

back and stretched her arms wide. Her body went rigid. An orange light began to throb in the middle of her chest, over her heart. It grew brighter, redder and darker, passing from orange to red to scarlet to purple, until at last the light glowed an intense blue, like the fiercest, hottest part of Dain's kiln.

Storm began backing away, stumbling over the churned shingle. She could not take her eyes off the Fire-witch. She grunted in disbelief as the ground beneath the Fire-witch erupted and Rekka rose into the air, standing on a churning column of fire.

Storm froze. She herself had ridden waterspouts. But she hadn't thought it possible… These thoughts took less time than the blink of an eye. Before she'd finished thinking them, she was moving. Scrambling, racing, and watching over her shoulder as the twisting column of fire lurched after her in a cloud of sparks and smoke, spitting charred stones as it rolled across the beach, spinning faster and faster. Chasing her. Catching her!

Frantic with the blind fear of prey that knows it is about to feel the claws and teeth of the predator, Storm headed towards the beach and the sea that might save her.

As she ran, Storm heard, for the first time, the sound

of her human audience. The Drowned Ones on the encircling ridge were screaming and hollering, frantic with excitement. She had time for one bitter thought – *At least we're providing them with good entertainment!* – and then she began to cough as smoke thickened the air. The earth was being torn apart behind her; explosions shattered the air as rocks burst in the heat.

Storm dared take one heart-stopping look behind her and gasped. The column of fire, now the height of a ship's mainmast, was nearly upon her. And riding on top of it was Rekka. The Fire-witch seemed to be in a trance of ecstasy, arms still outspread. But she was looking straight at Storm and, horrifyingly, her eyes had vanished, replaced by spinning circles of flame.

Storm ran even faster. The sea was her only hope. Rekka could not follow her there. The Drowned Ones wouldn't let her stay in the water, but if she swam fast enough, if she was lucky, perhaps she would find a way to fight, to survive.

Storm reached the shore, ran forward into the ferocity of the lashing waves, the howl of the wind in her ears. The seabed seemed to shelve here for a long way, the water too shallow for swimming. As Storm splashed and lurched towards the safety of deep water, she heard Rekka howl in fury.

Instinctively, she fell to her stomach and wormed forward beneath the water on hands and knees. A concussion battered the water, rocking her. She heard the sound of an explosion, then the hissing of a million snakes. The water around her began to heat; it felt as though she was inside a tea kettle about to come to the boil.

Frantically, Storm writhed and crawled. The water was cooler here. Nearly deep enough. Once she was swimming properly, she would circle the island and find a place where Rekka wouldn't see her crawl back on the land. It wasn't much of a plan, but it was all she had. Then her groping hands and pushing feet met emptiness and she fell into the caldera itself, tumbling down and down into the deep heart of the dead volcano.

15

Storm opened her eyes. In front of her, close enough to touch, huge and purple-grey, swam the Dolphin. It floated in blue-green water illuminated by streams of sunlight pouring down from the sky above the surface. This time there was no imagining. There was no doubt.

Storm swam closer to the Elemental until she was looking right into one of its enormous eyes. *I tried*, she thought at it. *I'm sorry I failed.* Then, for the first time in many long and lonely weeks, Storm heard the voice of the Dolphin inside her head.

You have not failed, Storm. Far from it. You have done just as we planned and hoped. Now it is time for you to engage with the Salamander's witch. But before we return your magic, remember, even if you should win this battle, you can still lose the war. A choice lies ahead of you. Choose well! Now grab my dorsal fin.

Quickly! The time is upon us!

She reached out both arms and grabbed hold of the fin rising from the upper part of the Dolphin's back. It felt warm, smooth and very real. It was taller than a house, but had a ropelike edge perfect for hanging on to. As soon as she took a firm grip, the broad back beneath her feet coiled, released and the Dolphin seemed to fly upwards through the water. She could feel every sideways stroke of its giant tail as the Dolphin shot towards the surface.

The water grew greener, sunlight streaming, lighting the way. She needed to breathe. Now! The Dolphin gave a last enormous thrash of its tail, and the Elemental and its human rider shot out of the sea high into the air.

To Storm's horror, at the top of its leap the Dolphin bucked, shrugging her off and sending her spiralling high into the air. She was too breathless even to scream. Her body reached the peak of its journey upwards and seemed to pause in mid-air. Then, arms and legs windmilling frantically, Storm began the long fall back towards the island.

Down and down she plummeted, tumbling head over heels. As she fell, Storm caught glimpses of Rekka's fire column moving over the island. By now Storm had gulped enough air. She screamed loud and long.

A dark shadow blotted out the sky. Enormous wings beat the air with a sound like the crack of thunder, drowning out her screams, the roar of the wind and the shouts of the Drowned Ones watching from the caldera's ridge.

Down draughts buffeted Storm, batting her back and forth through the air. Despite the chaos of fear in her head and the jumble of noise, Storm realised that the Albatross had arrived.

Enormous talons grabbed her round the middle like an eagle catching a dove. Her fall stopped with a force that winded her. And then she was no longer tumbling headlong, but being carried in a long, gliding, downwards spiral. Storm had a fraction of a moment to revel in the sensation of flight, then all her attention became focused on the fact that the tiny island where the Fire-witch waited was approaching with terrifying speed.

It is time, Storm.

She hadn't realised how much she had missed the Air Elemental's voice.

This is the moment that decides the future. Your magic was taken so we could reach this place, this time, these humans. Now that it is restored, use the powers of Air and Water wisely.

119

Remember the teachings of the Tortoise!

Those words were still ringing in her head when the Albatross folded its wings, barrel-rolled and plummeted earthwards. The force of the fall snatched most of the air from Storm's lungs and all the questions from her mouth.

The Albatross levelled off just before hitting the ground. Then they were skimming above the hard volcanic shingle of the island. Storm had a glimpse of a column of twisting fire before plunging into a cloud of steam. She smelled the bitter stink of scorched rock.

The Fire-witch and her destruction disappeared behind them as the Albatross circled the island. Without warning, the Elemental reared back with a giant flapping of wings and deposited Storm on the damp shingle. She dropped lightly to the ground and watched the Elemental circle once before flapping away. In a breath the Albatross was gone.

Was it magic she could feel thrilling her blood? Or the knowledge that the Tortoise, Albatross and Dolphin had not abandoned her – that she was no longer alone? Storm sprinted over the darkly shining shingle towards the wall of earth that the Tortoise had raised to protect Scoundrel.

The fire column had vanished. Where was her enemy? Where was Scoundrel? She wanted to make sure the cling-monkey was safe. But her first job was not to run headlong into an ambush.

The wind had died away. Storm heard distant shouts of Drowned Ones watching from the ridge. Had they seen the Elementals? If so, they would have a lot to think about! She wouldn't need to worry about interference from her captors any time soon. No sane person would want to be in the middle of the battle that was about to start.

A twisting knot in her stomach tightened. She had her magic back, but she hadn't used it for weeks. Magic was tricky. Then there was Rekka. The Fire-witch had just shown the devastating extent of her power. She was a monster – a human dragon!

Storm slowed to a trot as she approached the spot where she had last seen Scoundrel. She listened for the telltale crunch of shingle. Carefully, she approached the wall of magicked earth. There was no one hiding behind it. Storm climbed to its top, all attempts at self-concealment over. Where was Rekka? Had the Fire-witch somehow escaped the islet?

She slowly rotated, scanning every wet, rocky bit of land. With a shock of surprise, Storm saw a small canoe lying on its side on a tiny scrap of shingle. Someone had landed!

"Are you looking for me?"

Rekka! Storm whirled round. The Fire-witch had been lying in a shallow pit in the shingle. She jumped to her feet and laughed. Her tangled plaits of black hair fell over her shoulders like a mass of coiled snakes. Her scarlet tunic was smeared with ash and the dust of exploding shingle. Her face was soot-blackened. But her smile was viciously broad and toothy.

"Time we gave our audience what they're waiting for, don't you think?" The Fire-witch gestured to the ring of watching Drowned Ones, whose shouts were growing ever louder.

"I had my back to you. You could have attacked. Why didn't you?"

"That would have been too easy. I want to enjoy every moment of your fear. I want to drink in your desperation as you realise you can't defeat me. See your face when you realise death has come for you. I intend to kill you slowly, Storm. Bit by agonising bit. I will melt the skin from your flesh so delicately that you'll feel an eternity of pain in your last moments of life."

Storm winced at the force of the woman's spite. "Why do you hate me so much?"

"Hate gives me strength, child. It's you or me, and I intend to survive. Hate is my food and drink! But, that aside, I hate you because you deceived me, and I don't like being made a fool of! Today you actually managed to trick me into thinking you had lost your magic, right up to the moment when you used Earth magic to save the monkey. You devious little liar!"

Storm shook her head – the Earth magic had been nothing to do with her – but she didn't bother to argue.

The Fire-witch stood straighter. Her grin vanished and her long thin face became stern, even beautiful. For one quick heartbeat Storm caught a glimpse of the woman Rekka might have been. Slowly, the Fire-witch raised her hands over her head, taking her time, supremely confident.

Storm knew she had to fight; she had to win! She reached into the air with her mind and found Air music. Then, reaching to the waves now splashing gently against the island's shingled shore, she found Water music. Prickly, tingling magic began to build inside her body. Her skin felt hot and tight, as though the power shining inside would burst her apart.

When the Fire-witch attacked, Storm was ready.

Rekka pointed a long talon and, with a hiss like a giant snake, shot a thin condensed ray of fire from her finger. The ray flashed high into the air and coiled upwards, creating a noose of fire that began to descend towards Storm.

Storm didn't try to dodge. Instead, she sang out a single loud note. With the roar of a enraged bull, a wind came out of nowhere and dashed the rope of flame into a shower of sparks, then swept them away to drown in the sea. Storm panted from the effort.

Be ready, warned her mind-voice.

Rekka growled with frustration and immediately whipped a thick rope of fire at Storm's head. *So much for a slow death*, remarked her mind-voice, as Storm dodge-rolled in the nick of time and responded with a blast of her own, this time with wind so strong that the Fire-witch was plucked off her feet and thrown a canoe length along the beach.

Storm grinned, relieved to find that not only was her magic back, but it seemed stronger than ever! Perhaps this wouldn't take too long after all.

Don't get overconfident! warned her mind-voice. *The witch isn't finished yet.*

Rekka surged high into the sky, riding another tornado of fire. The fire column swept towards Storm, roaring as it churned over the shingle. The Fire-witch lashed out. The beach in front of Storm exploded in steam and smoke. Rocks catapulted high into the air. Storm ran for her life, dodging and stumbling over the uneven ground. And then she fell.

Rekka was on her in a heartbeat. Storm almost fainted from the intensity of the heat. The air itself was scorched – too hot to breathe, to call her magic, to save herself. The ground beneath her seemed to melt. She slid down into darkness.

16

Death seemed to be totally dark. That made sense, but it didn't make it any more pleasant. As she strained her eyes for any glimmer of light, Storm realised she still had eyes to strain – and skin and muscles that told her she was lying on something damp and hard. Something else, sharp and unforgiving, was prodding her in the back. It felt like a rock.

Storm soon had to admit that she was alive and didn't know whether to be happy or even more scared. Where was she? Wherever it was, the air was stuffy and smelled of rock and earth and mud. She tried to sit up and cracked her forehead against something hard. "Ow!"

The echo of her voice bounced back at once. She reached up and touched a solid mass barely a handspan above her. With growing panic, Storm felt everywhere she could reach. She tried to wriggle forward and hit a wall. The same behind.

She clamped a hand over her mouth and pressed hard. If she started to scream, she would not be able to stop. She was cocooned in the earth, buried alive! The Tortoise must have acted to save her at the last moment. But how was she supposed to get out? It was already hard to breathe. Even now the small amount of air that was left was growing warm and thick, hotter and hotter … too hot! Which meant…

The ceiling of earth over her head was beginning to glow red, like the inside of a clay oven. The Fire-witch had found her. And Rekka intended to bake her alive!

Storm clawed at the earth sealing her in the ground. She swore and snatched away her fingers – the soil was already too hot to touch. She bit her lower lip hard to stop the scream swelling in her throat. Blood trickled into the back of her mouth, making her gag. As she choked, the glowing shell of earth overhead cracked wide open and shattered.

Blinded by the glare of sunlight, Storm scrambled to her feet, gasping in fresh air, reaching for her magic as she did so. She could feel her skin shrink in anticipation of a blast of fire. Someone she couldn't see was shouting.

Several someones. She heard Scoundrel, shrieking at the top of his lungs. Her eyes struggled to adjust to the sudden glare of midday. The dull reddish brown of the shore appeared, and the intense blue of the sky, the sun a white ball of heat glowering overhead.

Figures strode across the shingle: one clad in scarlet shooting fire arrows from twitching talons; one deflecting each fire shaft with a spinning disc of earth that leapt from nimble fingers; one half crouched in the scant shelter of a hollow, bow stretched taut. And one monkey screeching curses from his perch on the neck of the Earth-witch.

"Nim!" Storm was surprised into a shout that distracted the Drowned One at a crucial moment. The disc of stone he had been magicking slipped from his fingers and shattered on the ground. At the same moment, Rekka lashed out furiously at him.

Nim dropped and rolled, dodging the blast by a finger's width. Scoundrel sprang sideways, leaping for his life, and Mer – for it was her – stood and loosed an arrow at the Fire-witch.

A great many things happened at once. Mer's arrow nicked Rekka's left arm, cutting a bloody channel in her flesh. Nim jumped up and began to sing, building his Earth magic for the next effort. And Scoundrel leapt on to a boulder and shrieked even more insults at the Fire-witch.

Air music screaming in her head, Storm called thunder as she ran towards the Fire-witch. A scowling cloud billowed overhead, shutting out the sun. Along with the gloom came a gust of wind born of her anger and fear. It lashed the island, threatening to knock the combatants off their feet.

A bit much, commented her mind-voice. *You always overdo it!*

Leaning into the wind, her hair streaming behind her and red tunic flapping, Rekka lashed out with a rope of fire, not at Nim or Storm, but at Mer! Nim shouted in defiance, and the earth in front of Mer rose in a tumbling, churning wall of stone and mud. Fire crashed into the wall and vanished in a hiss of steam and a crack of breaking stone. Mer wriggled backwards, then sprinted to shelter behind a rise of ground. Nim was shaking with effort, his face sweaty.

Storm sprinted towards the Salamander's agent. Rekka had her back to her, all her fury focused on Nim.

The Fire-witch was also panting with effort. She had snarled when she saw Mer escape. Now she attacked Nim, pelting handful after handful of fireballs at the Drowned One, who struggled to spin discs of earth fast enough to shield himself. He could not keep it up much longer. Sure enough, the disc he was making slipped from his fingers and splintered to stone fragments. Rekka hissed with laughter, taking her time, totally sure of herself. In her lust for revenge on the boy who had saved Mer, she seemed to have forgotten Storm completely.

"Enough!" Storm shouted, and the deluge began. Water poured from the sky. It was as though a celestial bath had been emptied on the caldera. Storm staggered under the force of the blow. She was immediately drenched to the skin, her hair plastered to her head.

Rekka screamed. Through the waterfall pouring over her face, Storm saw steam begin to pour off the Fire-witch. Her fireballs were extinguished mid-air.

Is it that easy? asked Storm's mind-voice. *Have we won?*

As though in answer, the ground at Storm's feet began to swell and heave. Storm stumbled back, her eyes jerked to Nim. Was this his doing? But the Drowned One was staring open-mouthed. And then he shouted, "Run, Storm! The volcano! The Salamander is reviving it! I can't stop it!"

Her breath dried in her lungs. Volcano! The greatest fear of all Islanders, even more than the tsunamis that regularly punished the easternmost islands. She began

130

to stumble backwards as panic took hold of her mind.

Nim darted forward, grabbed her by the arm and began to pull her towards the canoe. "We've got to get out of here! Now! Come on! Mer! Scoundrel!"

Storm struggled to clear the panic from her mind. What had the Albatross said? *This place, this time, these humans.*

"No!" She pulled away from the Drowned One. "We *can* win. We must! If we work together."

"I can keep the earth from rising into a volcanic cone, but I can't stop the magma forcing its way out! It's melting the rock as fast as I try to seal it over!" shouted Nim. He was panting with the effort of making magic and his eyes were wild. She remembered that it was his people who had most to fear from volcanoes. The Drowned Ones had nearly been wiped out by eruptions in the ancient war between the Elementals.

"The Dolphin will drown it!" she said. "Dig a channel. Carve the island in two and I will flood the centre!"

Nim's eyes widened with hope. He nodded and began to sing, gathering his magic. Storm saw sweat bead on his forehead.

"Watch out!"

Mer's voice made Storm whirl round just in time to

dodge a fire arrow. Rekka had survived the stormburst. Despite the howling wind and driving rain, the Fire-witch was growing stronger. Red-black magma oozed from a crack in the ground at her feet. Rekka stood knee-deep in a puddle of molten rock, not burning, not screaming in pain, but growing visibly stronger every moment. She yelled exultantly as her entire body began to glow the same black-red as the lava. It was as though her flesh had turned into living magma. Her skin seethed and erupted, black crusts crumbling and churning before sinking as fresh lava surged to the surface.

Storm felt bile rise in her throat. Rekka's eyes had become spinning pinwheels of flame, starkly staring from molten skin. Her bones seemed to melt and the witch's shape shifted and flowed. She stood astride a mini-pimple of a baby volcano.

"Not human," Mer muttered in Storm's ear.

"Go!" Storm shouted. "Get to the boat. Take Scoundrel and row out as far as you can. The island will not last."

"I'm not going without Nim." Mer was pale and shaking, but her stubbornness was intact and her eyes never left the Drowned One boy, who stood as if made of stone, eyes shut in concentration.

The island seemed to groan in pain as Nim's Earth magic bored through the rock beneath the shingle at the far end of the island. The new channel edged slowly from the beach towards the middle of the island, the sea churning impatiently in its path. The Fire-witch snarled and shot another fire arrow at them, which Storm deflected with a shield of spinning air.

Rekka's attack seemed to convince Mer. "I'll take the verminous creature to the boat, but we'll wait in the shallows until the two of you have finished." The Bellumer darted away to scoop a protesting Scoundrel from a nearby rock and – holding the monkey at arm's distance in front of her – raced to the canoe. She tossed Scoundrel aboard and pushed off.

With a sigh of relief Storm got back to the business of fighting. She had to fend Rekka off long enough for Nim to dig his channel. The witch was surging upwards, growing larger, looking as unstoppable as the magma oozing beneath the hillock she stood upon. Though she was several arrow lengths away, the stink of her made Storm want to vomit; it was an unholy mixture of burning sulphur and unwashed human.

Shock at Rekka's transformation had broken her concentration, and her cloudburst had dwindled to a mere drizzle. Now Storm called to the Albatross and the Dolphin. She must drench the island, batter the Fire-witch with wind and water. She found the place in her mind where the music of Air and Water were strongest, and moved between Nim and Rekka, in case the Fire-witch lashed out at him.

Storm timed her first attack to hit just at the moment when Rekka lifted her arm for another assault. A gust of wind struck the Fire-witch like a hammer blow, sending her reeling. She fell into the mouth of her mini-volcano and sank up to her neck in lava. Rekka's shriek of fury belched out a stinking cloud of black smoke that, even at that distance, made Storm gag.

Please, Storm prayed to her ancestors, *let her stay down. Let it be over.*

As if in answer, Rekka's arms surged up out of the lava and grasped the edges of the fire pit. Slowly, her body shedding charred fragments of rock, the witch rose clear.

Storm struck again, screaming with the effort of marshalling both wind and water. Her magic seized the next wave about to strike the island's shore. The magicked wave roared across the sea bed. When it reached the island, the wall of water was as tall as a ship's mainmast. Wind swooped, and the wave leapt up to meet it. Their collision formed an enormous sideways waterfall that soared blue-green, spitting fish and seaweed over Storm's head. The wave-waterfall struck the Fire-witch and knocked her off the cone of magma. Rekka tumbled head over heels inside the deluge of seawater as it washed over the islet.

Please, Ancestors, prayed Storm's mind-voice, *let that be an end!*

Sweating and panting with effort, Storm darted a glance at Nim. The Earth-witch was singing his Earth music in a low tuneful voice. He sounded tired and his breathing was laboured. But the channel he was carving was more than two-thirds of the way towards the mini-volcano, which still seeped magma from its mouth.

Storm felt a surge of hope. They might make it! The Dolphin prowled, and the sea lashed at the confines of the new canal, sending spray high into the air, as though chiding Nim to get on with it.

But when she looked back to her enemy, a mere heartbeat later, Storm cursed herself. The Fire-witch lived. Worse, Rekka had recovered to a horrifying degree. The Salamander's witch was once more clothed in her own flesh instead of magma. But skin that had been a rich amber was now the colour of dead straw. The hair had been scorched from Rekka's head.

Likewise, her tunic had burned to ash. The witch was naked, hairless, but alive.

The Fire-witch limped towards the pimple of rock oozing magma. Although she moved slowly, she seemed a force of nature, unstoppable. Her face a grimace of hate, she straddled the mouth of her volcano and raised her arms skyward.

Instead of a tornado of fire, Rekka called forth from the fiery depths a writhing tongue of molten rock. Purple-red and seething, shedding black scales of charred earth, the magma bore the Fire-witch high into the air. Storm readied herself for another blast of wind. She would knock Rekka off her column of lava before the witch could lash out at them. But to her horror, instead of merely lifting the Fire-witch into the air directly over the fire pit, the tongue of magma extended, rolling over the ground towards them like the body of a snake.

"She's figured out how to come for us," Nim shouted. He moved to stand beside her.

Storm clutched his arm. The boy was shaking. Whether from fear or exhaustion she couldn't tell. "Can you do it?"

"I have to, so I will." All the old stubbornness that had once so frustrated her was plain in his voice, and she couldn't help a quick smile. More surprising was the emotion that swept through her. Nim – her always enemy – had become her friend.

"So will I. But it's going to get a bit chilly!"

Letting go of Nim, she gathered every last bit of her concentration. She was going to attempt an ice storm. Only once before had she conjured an ice storm, and that had been by accident. It had blasted the Fire-witch nearly to her death. But there was a danger: the route to ice was through anger.

She made herself think of her mother lying dead in her arms. Then, as she fed her anger, she forced herself to remember the charred remains of the Fire-witch's victims. Rekka had killed too many. She was remorseless, evil! Storm would not let her kill Nim, Mer and Scoundrel. Her heart chilled, her anger exploded, and Storm felt the temperature of the air around her plummet. Nim swore under his breath, his teeth chattering.

"You are finished, Rekka! I have won!" Storm taunted the Fire-witch, leading her away from Nim.

Rekka snarled in answer, and the worm of lava writhed and coiled faster over the ground as the Fire-witch pursued her rival.

Storm turned her back on her enemy, knowing such

a sign of contempt would inflame Rekka to the point of madness. She strode towards the beach, her breath frosting the air. Snow began to fall, a swirling blanket of white. Ice encrusted her lashes. It began to form a skin on her torso, over her heart, on her arms, neck and legs. Storm was shivering violently, but still she walked.

Behind her, she heard Nim singing his magic. His song floated over the island. It seemed strangely pure and sweet music with which to go into battle. On Yanlin they had faced invaders to the sound of conch shells and drums. The shouts and cries of the watching Drowned Ones rumbled above them like the battle drums of her island.

Now! She turned to see Rekka surging towards her faster and faster, heedless of the snow and ice. Storm knew her enemy would try to strike first. *Let her try!* Storm fumed. *I will crush her!*

Beware! warned her mind-voice.

Ice is born in the cold bitter anger of the heart. But anger confuses and fury leads to risk-taking. Storm gasped. She had fooled herself into thinking she was invincible! She had forgotten the Tortoise's warning and let hatred infect her anger, been about to put all her effort into attack – foolish beyond words when facing such an enemy!

Chastened, Storm raced to the spot she had chosen for her attack: the shore, where waves lashed and pounded the shingle. She held the Tortoise's words in her mind and heart as she reached out for the coldest winds marshalled by the Albatross, the coldest depths of the Dolphin's domain, and spun them hard and fast into ice.

When she turned to face the Fire-witch, Storm was no longer prey. She was a hunter springing a trap, and the Dolphin swam at her back and the Albatross soared above.

17

At the sight of the pounding waves, the spray shooting into air high as the mast of a ship, Rekka reared back, her snake of lava coiling round and round. The Fire-witch hissed in disgust at the sight of the Element she feared. But she was mad with triumphant fury, heedless of danger.

"You have damaged me, Storm of Yanlin. But still you will lose! The Salamander has enough power now to defeat you, to defeat all three of the Elementals and their puny attempts to subdue him. Fools! To choose *you*. A mere child." Rekka raised both hands and pointed them at Storm. Her eyes were whirling discs of fire.

But even while the Fire-witch raged, Storm had been preparing her ice storm. Now it sprang from her heart and down ice-crusted arms and out through stiff near-frozen fingertips. Seawater leapt from the waves at her back, washed over her, froze into a beam of icy slush, made even colder by the sea's salt, and gushed from Storm's outstretched hands right at the Fire-witch.

Rekka had time only for a yowl of fear before the sea ice swallowed her. The witch staggered backwards, toppling off the coiling magma. She twisted and scrambled back towards the retreating flow lava, which had dwindled to ground level and was oozing back towards the crack in the middle of the island. Rekka waded into the fiery stream and washed the ice from her body with handfuls of molten rock, sending up hissing clouds of steam. She was shivering, drenched, and the coil of magma was retreating ever more quickly back to its source.

The blast of icy seawater had drained Storm's energy. She was shivering as violently as Rekka. She felt frozen through. But she couldn't afford to stop. If Rekka reached the infant volcano, she would find new reserves of strength. Storm prayed to the Ancestors: *Please, let Nim's channel be ready!* It was the only thing that would end this fight once and for all – that, or Rekka's death.

Storm fought exhaustion like an enemy as she

staggered after Rekka. There was no one else. She was the one the Elementals had Chosen. All four, it seemed. Storm shuddered, and this time it wasn't the cold that make her shiver. She broke into a run. She didn't have time to see how Nim was faring. It was now or never!

Storm focused as she ran. She closed on her enemy. Rekka was crawling rapidly towards the volcano's mouth, whimpering and cursing. The Fire-witch was only an arrow's flight from safety, but Storm was close enough! She dropped to her knees and used the last of her strength to channel her magic. She launched a final ferocious blast of ice. A spear of solid ice flew from her fingers. Spinning as it flew, glinting silver in the shafts of sunlight filtering through the fogs of dust and steam, the spear drove straight for the Fire-witch.

Storm did not see what happened next. She fell forward on to her face. She had spent all her power, all her magic, all her physical strength. She lay on the frozen shingle, cradling an aching head in cold-numbed hands.

A scream of agony erupted from the fire pit.

So, she had struck the witch.

A bellow of fury followed.

So, she had not killed the witch.

Then came a sound so amazing and terrifying that Storm found the strength to raise her head.

Rekka had managed to get to the fire pit before Storm's ice spear had struck her. Now she stood in the flow of welling lava, clutching her left arm. It hung wrongly, broken above the elbow. Shards of ice littered the ground around the witch, melting as Rekka began to drink in the power of the magma once more. The spear had wounded but not defeated her. The witch was beginning to glow red. Her flesh beginning to transform.

But the island itself was screaming, groaning, shuddering. Storm's heart pounded painfully and the ground heaved and shifted beneath her feet. All Islanders feared earthquakes. She pushed herself upright and turned to look for Nim.

The Drowned One stood like a statue, only his lips moving as his song of Earth magic began to swell. The channel had reached the fire pit. Rekka picked up a huge chunk of lava with her good hand and threw it at Nim. It hurled through the air, missing him by the span of a hand. The Earth-witch didn't flinch. He sang on, his voice growing louder, higher and higher, until it reached a long note of pure resonance. At that moment, the island shuddered. The earth gave an ear-piercing screech. Storm clapped her hands over her ears as Nim's magic ripped apart the remaining rock, and the sea, released at last, poured into the fire pit.

18

The Dolphin, having been frustrated in its fury for so long, showed no mercy. The first wave to escape the channel reared up five times the height of a human, and slammed down on the Fire-witch. Steam roiled and hissed as the wave swept over the surface of the island. Storm stood in water to her knees, struggling to stay on her feet. Then, with a huge sucking noise, the sea poured itself into the fire pit.

The explosion that shook the island made Storm's ears ring. The submerged surface of the island convulsed, like a rat shaking itself. Waist deep in water, Storm stared in awe as a column of steam burst from the fire pit, shooting high into the air. As fast as the Salamander's lava turned the water to steam, even more water poured in, flooding, drowning. At last the steam geyser faltered; the column of steam dwindled, sank and died. The sea had won. The fire pit was flooded to the rim. Its job done, the Dolphin returned to its element, and the surface of the island slowly reappeared.

Storm looked for Nim. The boy was standing, amazed, as if in a state of shock. She ran to him. "You did it!"

"*We* did it. Rekka would have killed me if you hadn't stopped her. Is she dead?" He gestured, and Storm turned round to see a body lying in a crumpled heap. The giant wave had tossed the Fire-witch halfway across the island.

"I'll see." Storm started to run to the witch, but Nim grabbed her arm.

"Leave her. We've got to get to the canoe and get out of here."

"What?"

"Have you forgotten my people? How do you think Mer and I got here?"

"They won't dare attack. Not after what they've just seen."

"Don't count on it!" snapped Nim. "I've betrayed my tribe. There is no greater sin. They could try to ambush us. Enough arrows and—"

"We'll deal with it. I'm checking Rekka!" Storm pulled her arm away. "Are you coming?"

Nim frowned with frustration, and she saw the marks of exhaustion on his face. And something else. She had seen loss often enough to recognise it.

"Let's get on with it then!" Nim loped across the shingle to the Fire-witch's body. Storm ran faster and beat him there. Rekka lay face down. She wasn't moving, but Storm saw her sides move slowly in and out. The Fire-witch was alive. She was also beginning to shiver uncontrollably as shock set in.

Storm whipped off her over-tunic and laid it over the Fire-witch's body. The woman growled, tried to push herself up and hissed in pain.

"Lie still," Storm said. "Your arm is broken. You need a healer."

But the Fire-witch pushed herself to sitting. She clutched Storm's tunic round her. "The cold... I dreamed that I was back..." Her eyes were half closed, her face grey, her left arm hung useless. The wrongness of its shape made Storm's stomach squirm.

Rekka slowly shook her head, as if to clear it. She looked up and recognised Storm. She glared and the pupils of her eyes began to glow red. "I will kill you!"

"Not today," said Storm.

"Come on!" Nim had arrived. He tugged at Storm's shoulder. He was staring at the Fire-witch in fascinated disgust.

Storm had to admit the woman looked dreadful: her hair singed from her head and her skin a sickly grey. She looked ill, and much, much older. The Fire-witch had paid a high price for her magic.

"If not today," said Rekka, "there is tomorrow!" She ignored Nim, watching Storm as though memorising every line of her face. "And if not tomorrow, then the next day, or the next. However long it takes, I will kill you, Storm of Yanlin. Be sure of that!"

"She's right," Nim said. "As long as the witch lives, both you and the Balance are under threat. I'll finish her now!" He put his hand to his belt and drew his knife.

Rekka looked at him and laughed. "You haven't the courage!"

"Wait…" Storm said. Nim was wrong. Killing Rekka now, when she could not fight back, would be simple murder. "Don't hurt her!" She grabbed Nim's knife arm.

"But…"

"It's another way for the Salamander to win! If we kill her while she's helpless, we feed Fire with the hate it craves."

"But this is different!"

"I don't think so."

Nim glanced at Rekka and frowned. He pressed his lips into a grim line and slid his knife back into its sheath. "Maybe you're right. We had better leave at once. In case you haven't noticed, the Drowned Ones are moving off the heights."

The Drowned Ones, noted Storm's mind-voice. *Like he's not one of them any more.*

"Come on!" Nim grabbed Storm by the hand and they fled, racing over the shore to the waiting canoe. Mer was already poling towards deeper water. Storm splashed through the shallows ahead of Nim and held the boat steady while he hauled himself over the side. He held out his hand and pulled her aboard. Mer, her face grim, began to paddle at once. Nim took up the second paddle and the canoe glided quickly round the island towards the entrance to the caldera.

"Too late," said Nim. He stowed his paddle and stood to face his newest enemy.

In front of them, blocking the narrow entrance, were a dozen Drowned One canoes, each one full of archers standing ready with bows drawn and arrows notched.

19

"Surrender, Earth-witch!" Peggot stood in the foremost canoe. She pointed her wooden staff at Nim. "Traitor to your own. You must face the council of Elders and your just punishment."

Storm reached out and pulled Nim back down on to his seat. "I'll deal with this." She stood and faced Peggot. "I sank one of your raft towns in Yanlin harbour, Peggot. Do you think a few canoes will stop me?"

"My business is with Nim, witch," snapped the Elder.

"And mine is with you! I know you hate me for the death of your brother. I am sorry for his death, but you invaded us. If there is fault or guilt, it is yours, not mine. As for Nim, he answers to a greater authority – the Tortoise. You know full well witches are not subject to tribal loyalties, either to island or raft town. We are Children of the Elementals."

"I will not—"

"Silence!" roared Storm. She startled herself. Peggot stood open-mouthed. "Do not interrupt me again!" Storm warned. "Despite your grievance towards me, you have witnessed enough here today to realise that what Nim and I have told you is true: the Salamander seeks to destroy the Balance!

"Nim and I stand between you and more death than you can imagine. Death of your tribe, death of the seas, death of the islands you long to possess. Think on that, Elder!

"We are leaving this place. The battle with Fire is not yet won. I give you fair warning! If you try to stop us, I will sink every one of your canoes. I may sink your entire raft town if you rile me enough!"

"Holy Ancestors!" muttered Mer, staring at Storm in amazement. "I didn't think you had it in you. I begin to believe you myself!"

Nim just stared, stony-faced, at his Elder. Storm could not read what was in his mind, but she doubted his thoughts were happy ones.

Peggot thumped her staff on the deck of her canoe in frustration. Even from the distance of an arrow shot, Storm could see that the Elder was fuming. And unrepentant. Nothing she had said about greed and the Balance had made any impact on the old woman. But fear had.

Peggot might overcome an Earth-witch in the middle of the sea, but she had no chance against a Weather-witch. Grudgingly, the Elder turned away and shouted to her warriors. "Weapons down. Back to the town! Now!"

As the archers un-notched arrows and unstrung bows to take up paddles, Peggot turned once more to face them. "Nim, you have disobeyed your Elders, attacked one of your own clan, aided and abetted an enemy of the Drowned Ones. You are from this day no longer a Drowned One! You are cast out from the Dolphin Tribe! You are a No-thing and worse than a No-thing – you are Unclean! If ever you meet any of our tribe, they will smite you. Your death is hereby decreed!"

Storm put a hand on Nim's shoulder. He did not respond, not even to shrug it off. The Earth-witch merely stared at Peggot, his face pale, jaw clenched tight. Storm saw his hand gripping the oar begin to shake.

"Row!" Storm ordered Mer. "Let's get away from

here." She found a strand of Water music floating in the back of her mind, and set a current to push their canoe quickly through the water.

They soon hit the choppy water of the Inner Sea. Storm had escaped Rekka and the Drowned Ones at last, but she and her companions were alone in a small canoe far from help. There seemed only one place they could go. They had to try to reach the dubious safety of Bellum Island.

Storm set their easterly course as well as she could, calculating their position from the sun. She didn't know this part of the Inner Sea. She magicked a steady current flowing from the west, then set about smoothing the waves in front of their heavily laden canoe. Mer had taken the tiller, as if by right. She seemed lost in thought. As for Nim...

The Drowned One sat motionless, looking out to sea at nothing in particular. It seemed an impossible undertaking to pretend to be alone in a cramped canoe filled with two other humans and a cling-monkey, but he was doing his best.

Scoundrel crept quietly forward bit by bit until he sat as close as he could to Nim without actually touching him. From time to time the monkey gave a quiet whimper. The only other sounds were the thud and splash of waves against the hull of the canoe and the shriek of ever-present gulls hunting overhead.

The sun was beginning the slow journey to its bed beneath the sea at last, but it was still high in the sky and its heat was fierce. At first Storm welcomed the warmth, which soaked away the last of the bone-deep chill from magicking the ice storm. Soon, however, she was longing for a sun hat and water to drink. But since Nim had just lost everything he loved in order to rescue her, she didn't quite like to ask if he had thought to bring a water jar with him. So she swallowed the dryness in her mouth, grabbed up the bailing bucket and began scooping water from the deck and pouring it overboard. She was too tired to even think of using magic to do the job.

When Storm ran out of water to bail and slumped back in her place, Mer broke the silence. "Um … shouldn't we be celebrating? I mean, we're all alive at least."

Nim said nothing. Mer tried again: "I say we break out the water and seaweed cakes!"

"Water?" Storm sat upright. "Are you kidding? You two were clever enough to remember to bring water in the middle of an escape attempt?"

"Water *and* seaweed cakes," Mer said smugly.

"Personally, I think eating seaweed is overrated, but considering the circumstances I won't complain. Nim, would you mind fetching them out of the store, please?"

Storm blinked: *Mer, using tact instead of presumption? Whatever next?*

The Bellum girl continued to hold the rudder steady as she leaned forward and regarded Nim with an expression that showed actual concern. Storm wondered what had gone on between the two of them when Rekka had been interrogating her. It looked like real friendship, at least on Mer's part.

Roused from his dark thoughts at last, Nim nodded and moved to the bow where he pulled a water bottle and packet from the storage area. "Sorry," he said. "I haven't been much use… Shall I take the rudder while you have some food, Mer?"

"Yes, please!" Mer's voice was tart, but she smiled at Nim as he handed her the supplies before easing past to take the rudder oar.

Mer poured water into a coconut half and held it out to Storm, who took it with a polite bow of the head. She was still trying to figure out where Mer stood in all this, now that the Bellumer had escaped the Drowned Ones. What would the rebel do now her father was avenged and Waffa was dead? Return to her home island and continue the rebellion against the Pact, no doubt. But without, thank the Ancestors, the help of the Drowned Ones. All-out war had been averted, at least for a time.

The water was stale and tasted of seaweed, but Storm could have drunk ten times as much. "We need to head for Bellum," she said. "You and I, Nim, should try to contact Linnet. I suppose you −" she frowned at Mer, remembering how the Bellumer had treated the witches − "will agree to release the two men who helped you rescue me?"

"I'm sure," Mer said with a raised eyebrow, her tone as smoothly confident as ever, "that we can come to an arrangement that will help all of us. But if we want to get to Bellum any time soon you need to head a hand's width more northerly, Nim."

Nim shrugged. "I wouldn't know," he said in a monotone. "I don't know these waters."

"Well, I do!" Mer indicated a distant trio of islets on the northern horizon. "Those are the Triplets. Treacherous if you sail at night. We're too far south of them. Bellum is that way." She pointed. "If Storm can keep that current pushing us at this speed, we should get there before sun's end."

Nim changed course without further comment. But

Mer wasn't giving up on him. "Why don't you eat now, and I'll take over again?" She held out the packet of seaweed cakes.

Nim shook his head. "Not hungry."

Mer sighed but kept her silence. Storm watched her thoughtfully. The Bellumer had deflected her question neatly. Mer didn't want to talk about whatever plans she might be hatching. That was enough to make Storm suspicious.

"Mer's right," she said to Nim. "You need to eat something. And have a drink. You've never done magic that big before. It's exhausting and you have to keep strong. The Tortoise would—"

"Don't lecture me about the Tortoise!" Nim's apathy evaporated. He leapt to his feet, abandoning the tiller.

Mer raised an elegant eyebrow, then slipped into his place and took up the tiller. Her eyes darted between Nim and Storm, a look of anticipation on her face.

Nim glared at Storm. "I know my duty! Haven't I just demonstrated it? And it's lost me…" His mouth snapped shut, but his jaw moved as if he was chewing on words he wanted to say but would not.

"I'm sorry," Storm said cautiously. "I know I can't begin to imagine what you're feeling. But I do know what it is to lose the thing you love best." This wasn't going well, but things had to be said. She gathered her courage. "The fact is, we need you, Nim – me and Linnet and all the witches opposing the Salamander. We need you to be well. To be with us. We haven't won. You know that."

"You don't understand!" Nim said. "I was the orphan, the outcast! Ever since I can remember, I've only wanted one thing – to be part of my tribe! To be accepted. And now…"

"Sometimes the price for belonging is too high," Storm said, remembering the time they had met on her island, when she had saved his life and he had repaid her kindness with betrayal. "You sacrificed me and my cousin for your tribe once. I'm just glad that this time the Tortoise was able to convince you that other things are more important!"

Nim grunted as though she'd hit him. But she watched his anger fade. The Drowned One looked her squarely in the eyes. "You're right. I've never apologised properly for what I did to you and Minnow. I … I preferred to think I had no choice. But I did. It was just that it was hard, and I chose the easy way. I'm sorry."

Storm couldn't speak. She just nodded her thanks, her eyes full of tears.

"Well," snapped Mer. "Aren't the two of you just so

cute and cosy? But we still have quite a few problems. And the first one is getting safely to Bellum and landing without the Pact finding out I'm back. And you, I guess." She raised an eyebrow at Storm.

"Um," said Nim. "We have a more pressing problem than that."

"What?" Storm and Mer cried in unison.

"Off the starboard bow. See? Just rising on the second wave from the horizon. Unless I'm very mistaken, that's a Drowned One canoe!"

20

"Looks like it's on its own." Storm squinted into the distance. The sun was skimming above the waves directly over the foreign boat. But even through the glare, she could see a dark object bobbing up and down, disappearing in a trough and sweeping into view on the next wave.

"Hmmm," said Nim. "It's drifting all right. I wonder…" The Drowned One cast a quick glance at Mer, who was sitting still as a statue. Storm could tell the same thought had crossed the older girl's mind: they might have found Waffa's canoe.

"We have to check," Storm said, and adjusted the current to aim for the drifting boat. They began to go round in circles. The Bellumer had pushed the tiller hard to one side. "Stop it, Mer!"

"We're not going!" Mer said. "It's pointless. Besides, we have to get to Bellum by nightfall and it's getting late. Have you seen the sun?"

"Overruled, Mer. Two to one." Nim stood up and gestured to the Bellumer to relinquish the tiller. "I'll take the helm."

Mer glared at him before shifting her glare to Storm. Then she shrugged her shoulders, feigning indifference. "As you like." She pushed past Nim, her face furious. "Even if it is Waffa, it's too late. She must be dead. And I'm glad!"

As they drew nearer, Storm watched the drifting canoe bobbing and swirling. It was impossible to see if anyone was in the boat. Or even if it was the same canoe that had carried Waffa to her death.

If it was … *Ancestors*, Storm prayed. *Let her be alive!* She didn't like Waffa, but hate was the Salamander's source of strength, and if Mer had succeeded in causing her mother's death, Fire would grow even stronger.

As their canoe breasted the last wave, Storm stopped her Water magic. Nim used the last of the momentum to guide their boat until their bow nudged the other craft.

No one spoke. The canoe was the one that Waffa had been set adrift in, and the woman was still aboard.

Every time the waves raised their canoe, the huddled shape of a woman was clearly visible lying face down in the bottom of the boat. Storm and Nim exchanged glances. It wasn't safe to leave Mer alone in their canoe. That meant only one of them could investigate Waffa's fate.

"I'll go," Storm said. As she rose to her feet and made her way towards the bow, Storm cast a glance at the older girl. Mer sat with her fists clenched. She was looking out to sea. She continued to stare into the distance as Storm hitched the other canoe's painter to the gunnels and pulled Waffa's canoe into position. She hurdled both sets of gunnels and, with a knot of tension twisting her stomach, knelt to check the body of the Pact's tally-keeper.

A water bottle lay beside the body, uncorked and empty. Storm reached out and touched the back of Waffa's neck. It was raging hot! Her fingers searched and found a pulse. The heartbeat tripped like hammer blows, too fast, sometimes faltering beneath her touch. The woman lived, but she was suffering from heatstroke. And there was no room for her on their already overcrowded canoe.

Storm reached for her Air magic. Her reserves of energy were nearly gone, and each use of magic was more difficult, but Waffa had to be cooled down at once. White wisps thickened overhead and quickly grew into a small, dark-bottomed rain cloud that hovered over the two canoes. With a tiny crack of lightning and a baby rumble of thunder, rain poured from the cloud on to Waffa's canoe.

"What is it?" Nim called. He was standing, trying to see what was going on. Mer gave up her pretence of ignoring her mother's fate and jumped to her feet as well, making the canoe wobble violently.

"She can't still be alive!" Mer cried.

"Heatstroke." Storm ignored Mer and spoke to Nim. "I'll have to stay aboard this canoe and keep her wet. Throw me the water bottle and the bailing bucket."

Before Nim could move, Mer leapt forward and snatched the water bottle from the storage hatch. "She's not having any!" she shouted, holding the bottle out over the choppy waves.

Scoundrel began shrieking in protest, scolding the Bellum girl, who ignored him. Nim quickly lashed the tiller into position and stood up, obviously intending to try to grab the bottle from Mer.

"Try and I'll drop it," she warned him.

"Wait!" Storm said. "Mer, you have to do the right thing now. What your mother did was wrong—"

"She destroyed the only person I ever loved! You never met him. My father wasn't like the others born into the Pact. He wasn't selfish or greedy or downright evil! He cared about justice and fairness. He wanted to change Bellum, to share wealth with the ordinary people – those who actually made things! He wanted to reform the Pact and trade fairly with other islands instead of taxing them into poverty and dependence. He wanted a better world, and she killed him for it – for being a decent human being! She *deserves* to die!"

"That isn't your call," Nim said. "Let the people of Bellum decide. If she survives, put her on trial. A fair trial, mind. Keep her blood off your hands, or you're little better than she is."

"What?" Mer rounded on him. "A Drowned One preaching peace? You lot are experts in revenge and murder!"

"And look where it's got us," Nim said. "Revenge killing just makes more death, more killing. You're proof of that."

"Preach on, pirate!" Mer said, her voice cold. "It changes nothing. I promise you, I *will* kill her!"

Storm gave up trying to convince Mer – the girl was obsessed. Instead, she held Waffa's empty water bottle up to catch rain. It filled quickly, and Storm corked it and set it aside. Rainwater collected in the hull of the canoe and the tally-keeper was soon lying in a puddle of cool water. Storm turned the woman face up before the water grew deep enough to drown her.

"Give me your tunic!" she said to Nim, who unbuttoned his sleeveless overshirt and handed it to Scoundrel. The cling-monkey easily leapt across the gap between the boats with the tunic tucked under one arm. He dropped the clothing and crouched at her feet, glaring at Mer and muttering under his breath.

Storm folded Nim's tunic and tucked it beneath Waffa's head. Then she turned to look at Mer. "Are you going to help us get her to Bellum?"

"No!"

Storm shrugged. "We'll do it without you." She dismissed the thundercloud, attached the canoe's rope to the stern of Nim's canoe and nodded at the Drowned One. "I'll tend Waffa. The bilge water will keep her cool, and I'll give her a drink when she improves enough to take it. You head for Bellum."

Mer made no move to interfere. Storm found enough endurance to magic a current to push them through the seemingly endless waves of the Inner Sea. They kept the Triplets hard on their right and headed due east. Waffa lay in the cool rainwater that had collected in the belly of the canoe. The Bellumer looked seriously ill. It would be a close thing whether or not the woman lived.

Please keep her alive, Ancestors! Storm prayed. She didn't know why she felt Waffa's survival was important in the battle against the Salamander, but she grew sure of it when Scoundrel – who had no reason to love a woman who had kicked him only a few days before – crouched beside Waffa and repeatedly dipped his cupped hand into the puddle of rainwater in order to dribble water over the woman's hot forehead.

The sun touched the western horizon, floating on the surface of the sea. Soon it would plunge into the watery depths. A golden wash of light spread over the water in front of them, like a path. And now Storm began to recognise the islets and rocks they slowly sailed through. They were nearing Bellum.

Darkness at sea fell swiftly. A green flash and gloom was upon them.

"We don't dare risk the harbour," Nim said. "Not with a half-dead tally-keeper as cargo. And I doubt they'd give a Drowned One a warm welcome, even one who's been exiled. We'd best make for the island where I … uh…"

"Where you kidnapped me," Storm said tartly. "And

I agree. No public entrance. I don't think any of us are held in favour by the Pact. Even you, Mer."

"Especially not me," Mer said, breaking her long silence. "The Pact have declared me a class-traitor and put a bounty on my head. Where is this island?"

"Can you remember the way?" Storm asked Nim. "In the dark?" Waffa was beginning to moan and toss her head from side to side. She didn't know if it was a good or bad sign.

"Drowned Ones can find any place they've sailed to before, in the dark if necessary." Nim's voice was matter of fact, not boastful.

"Good! You take over." Storm released her magic with a sigh of relief. Waffa groaned more loudly and tried to raise her head. Scoundrel retreated with a chirp of alarm, then leapt back on to Nim's boat.

"Keep still!" Storm located the water bottle in the semi-darkness by touch and held it to Waffa's parched lips. The woman's eyes flickered; she sucked greedily. "That's enough. Not too much at first." Storm eased her back down on the pillow of Nim's tunic. "Stay still, Waffa. Rest. All will be well." She glanced up to see Mer watching them. In the gloom she couldn't see the expression on the older girl's face. Waffa might survive heat stroke and dehydration, but Mer would kill her mother if the opportunity arose.

Many heartbeats later, Nim guided his canoe through a channel between rocky pointed mini-islands towards a dark mass bigger than the others. Soon both canoes were making the familiar sound of a hull splashing through shallow water. Ahead, in the darkness, she saw Nim leap out and wade through waist-high water towards a dimly visible shore. She heard the crunch of sandals on shingle. They had arrived. And Waffa was still alive. For now.

21

"We got this far," Nim said. "But what now?"

They had dragged both canoes up the gently shelving beach to a safe place above the high-water mark and were sitting on the sand, resting. Waffa lay nearby on a pile of seaweed, where she would be cooled by the onshore breeze, and where one of them could keep an eye on her. Mer was seated on a large rock on the other side of the beach, as far from her mother as it was possible to get.

"How do we get to the main island?" Nim asked. "Or do we send a messenger?"

"Scoundrel knows," Storm said. "Look at him."

"Scoundrel?" Nim squatted down in front of the cling-monkey, who was swaying from side to side with impatience. The monkey took his hand and led the boy to the tall cliff fencing off the bit of shoreline, to the spot where water emerged from a cave entrance. It formed a large stream that oozed and trickled over a boggy bit of beach before emptying into the sea.

"He seems to want us to go into that cave." Nim grabbed the monkey and deposited him on his shoulders. "That's where you and he came floating out. Is there a way back to Bellum Island from here?"

"Yes. The stream starts inside another cave on Bellum. I could magic the canoe to take us upstream and try to find that cave. But it's risky. The underwater river leads to a vast lake. I'm not sure I remember the way. We could get lost. And then there's Mer and Waffa. They can't be left alone together." She darted a quick look at Mer but the Bellum girl had not moved.

"Yes, you're right there," Nim said. "Can you magic both canoes through? You must be pretty exhausted."

"I don't think we have any other choice."

←——→

It was Nim who decided to leave Mer unsecured. The only spare rope was the anchor rope for his canoe, and he refused to cut it up in order to tie her hands. "We may need it! Besides, she won't try anything." Since Mer seemed to have sunk into apathy, not looking or talking to either of them, and avoiding even looking at her mother, Storm had thought it safe to agree.

It happened after they had travelled far beneath the earth, deep into the magical space of the underwater lake. Tired as she was, Storm felt her heart soar at the sight of thousands of points of green light illuminating the velvet black above them. The glow-worms of Bellum's cave system sparkled like green stars in a midnight sky.

"Amazing!" Nim said, his voice ringing and echoing in the silence. The only other sound was the gentle lap of water against the canoe hulls as Storm magicked them across the vast lake. The last time, the Dolphin had guided her canoe. There was no sign of the Elemental now, but she thought she remembered the way, and Scoundrel seemed happy enough. If she started to head in the wrong direction, the Tortoise's emissary would let her know.

All was peaceful. Even Waffa seemed to have settled into a more natural sleep. Storm began to hum softly under her breath, murmuring the liquid tunes of the Water magic that propelled them.

The silence was broken by a sickening thud followed by a groan, and the sound of a body slumping on to a deck. Scoundrel began to screech.

"Nim!" Stormed cried. But the only answer was a

splash as someone dived into the water.

"Nim?" Storm listened to the silence of the cave, her skin prickling with anxiety. She heard the slosh of the other canoe as it slowly rocked to and fro in the black water. That and Scoundrel's cries of distress. "Quiet, Scoundrel!" Storm snapped. To her amazement the monkey fell silent at once.

"Mer?" she called to the darkness. "What have you done?"

A stealthy splash somewhere close. In the echoey space it was impossible to judge which direction the sound came from. Mer was circling the canoes. She intended to kill her mother, and it seemed that she didn't care who she hurt in her quest for vengeance. Storm broke out into a cold sweat as she thought about the sounds she had heard.

Storm struggled to control a mouth-drying fear that Nim was dead. She had to listen, to think. Lashing out and getting it wrong wouldn't help him. She felt for Waffa with one hand. The woman was unconscious, which was a blessing right now. But there was no way of chasing Mer down without leaving Waffa unguarded, even with Scoundrel to cry alarm. In the dark, Mer might get aboard and kill her mother before Storm could stop her. No. She would have to wait for the other girl to attack.

"Mer!" Storm shouted. "If you have harmed Nim, I will leave you here to drown! Didn't think about that, did you?"

"I did." Mer's voice, disembodied, echoed through the dark. It bounced off the water that mirrored a thousand green sparks floating in total indifference to the fate of the four humans acting out a drama in their dim light. "But you're too soft to do it. That's where we differ."

"We differ on many subjects," Storm replied, turning her head, trying to locate the direction of the voice. It was impossible: the cavern was too big and echoey. "Like murder."

"Justice isn't murder!"

"If you kill your mother, it will be revenge, not justice. If you want justice, let us take her to stand before the Elders of Bellum."

"The Pact? That's a joke. They're the ones who killed my father!"

"Not the Pact, Elders. Proper Elders, like the goldsmith I met in the market. If Nim is all right, I promise to help you remove the Pact from power peacefully. Then the ordinary people of the island can choose their Elders by a free vote. Just the way it happens on every other island."

"Nim will be all right." Mer's voice was softer … almost a whisper. Which meant…

Before Storm could react, the other girl grabbed the side of Storm's canoe with both hands and surged upwards, using all her body weight to tip the canoe over.

Storm lunged to the other side in an attempt to balance the boat, but it was too late.

Mer's side of the canoe dipped below the water line and proceeded to flip completely over on to its belly, emptying its contents into the cold lake water. Storm half leapt, half swam, reaching for Waffa as the unconscious woman slid out of the canoe. In the near darkness, lit only by the green glow-worm light, Storm saw the woman slip into the black water and disappear.

22

Knowing it was too late, Storm dived after her. She made herself relax and drift. Her only chance of finding Waffa before she drowned was if a current in the lake carried her in the same direction.

And then, like a silver sun rising, a light appeared ahead of her. It solidified and became the shape of the Dolphin. But a Dolphin the like of which she had never seen before. The Elemental glowed silver-blue, brighter than any phosphorescence. The light flowing from its body shone on something in the water. It was Waffa, drifting motionless a short distance from her.

Sending her silent thanks to the Water Elemental, Storm swam faster than she had ever done in her life. She grabbed Waffa beneath the arms and kicked for the surface. In a heartbeat they broke through the surface of the lake. Storm gulped in air, trying to make as little noise as possible as she struggled to locate Mer in the glow-worm dusk of the cave. She must be prepared to fend off a second ambush. As she trod water, clinging to the dead weight of the unconscious woman, the sound of splashing and swearing echoed around the cavern. Storm thought she heard Mer's voice. What was going on? Suddenly, Waffa came to life with a strangled gasp. The woman convulsed and began to lash out. Storm was so busy trying to keep Waffa from drowning them both that she barely noticed that the distant shouting and splashing had stopped until a voice rang out in the darkness.

"Storm? Over here!"

Storm gasped in relief. "Nim! Thank the Ancestors! But I could use some help!" Waffa was thrashing and struggling. Just as Storm thought she must let go or drown with her, the tally-keeper collapsed and became a dead weight once again. "Nim?" Storm called. "Where are you? Are you all right?"

"Sore head and feeling pretty stupid, but I'm fine," said Nim. "Keep talking and I'll find you." A splash of an oar, the swoosh of a hull carving through water, and Storm saw a dark shape loom over her, outlined in a faint green glow of phosphorescence. A hand reached down and gripped Waffa by an arm. Storm grabbed the gunnels with one hand and together she and Nim managed to haul and push the tally-keeper aboard.

"You'll have to stay in the water, I'm afraid," Nim said. "Hold on to the painter rope and I'll tow you."

"The other canoe?"

"Gone to the bottom I guess. No sign."

"Mer? Is she…?"

"That one?" Nim gave a harsh laugh. "She's trussed tight with the anchor rope and lying cosy next to her ma in the belly of the canoe. I reckon she's mad as a hornet and that suits me fine!"

"Are you all right? I heard a thud. Did she knock you out?"

"Stunned me. Hit me with the spare oar. I never saw that coming, more the fool. Trusted her not to attack me. I won't make that mistake again!"

Nim sounded disgusted, whether with Mer or himself Storm couldn't tell.

"I'm well enough," he said. "Here's the rope." Nim had been busy untying the painter from the bow and reattaching it to the stern. Now he threw it to Storm, who caught it and looped it under her arms with a hitch knot. "Will you manage?"

"I'll float on my back and let you do all the work,"

Storm said. "I'm looking forward to it!"

"Just don't fall asleep and drown yourself."

"Sleep is the last thing on my mind!" she said. Relief buoyed her, making her feel almost giddy. The worst was over! Waffa was alive and Mer restrained.

Soon she was drifting in cool lake water behind Nim's canoe, watching the glowing green lights glisten and glimmer overhead, listening to the Drowned One hum under his breath. Cut off from an upper world of worries, forgetting her promise to Nim, Storm drifted off to into a half-sleep.

A Dolphin, shining with its own light, swam beside her in her dreams, which seemed to last a lifetime and no time at all. Later she could not remember any of them – only the blue-silver glow of the Elemental spirit. She woke when she hit her head on something wooden and damp – the stern of Nim's canoe.

"Ah, Storm!" said a familiar voice. "It gives me great pleasure to see you again. Here, let me help you out of your predicament."

Linnet the Earth-witch splashed through the shallows lapping the shore of the underground lake, seized a dazed Storm by her arms, and helped her to stand. "Welcome once again to Bellum Island!"

←——→

"She will live."

The anxiety that had been building as soon as she saw the old Earth-witch emerge from the door of his tiny hut and move purposefully towards her vanished at once.

Waffa had settled into a deep state of unconsciousness after nearly drowning. She had not roused at all during the long and bumpy trip in a handcart from the warehouse district of Bellum Town to Linnet's home on the fringes of the city. Nothing had roused her, and Storm, who had seen these sort of not-sleeps before, had known it could end in the tally-keeper's death.

She had sat on the terrace of Linnet's garden, shaded by palm trees, surrounded by birdsong and the countless small animals that lived there, since she had woken at daybreak from a restless sleep. The sun had risen several hands into the sky and she had finished her breakfast some time ago.

Scoundrel had kept her company all morning, and now she hugged the cling-monkey so tightly he squawked in protest and leapt from her lap. "Sorry, Scoundrel!" She smiled at the old Earth-witch, who beamed at her for a moment. Then his face became grave.

"Waffa will make a full recovery, given enough rest

and nourishment. But her daughter…"

"What? Mer isn't ill?"

"She does not suffer from an illness of the body. But something has happened to her."

"Yes!" Storm indulged her anger for a moment. "She tried to murder her own mother!"

"Indeed." Linnet raised one eyebrow, and Storm knew she had been rebuked. She bowed her head in apology.

"It is true," said the Earth-witch, "that the will to commit matricide has long dwelt in Mer's heart and mind, like a worm corrupting the wholesomeness of an apple. But something happened to Mer last night, during her attempt to drown Waffa. She will not speak of it, but the girl is frightened and unsure. Her new-found vulnerability presents both danger and opportunity. I cannot say strongly enough how important it is that she renounce her murderous intention and hand her mother over to appropriate justice."

"And you want me—"

"To convince her, yes."

"I've tried and failed more than once." Storm sighed, thinking of Mer's stubborn self-belief. Something very extraordinary would have to have happened if she was to have any chance of success. A fool's errand, but it would be rude to refuse. "Very well, Linnet. I will go now. Where is she?"

"She's keeping her mother company."

Storm could not prevent her look of amazement.

The Earth-witch chuckled aloud. "Do not worry, child. I have my reasons. Go now."

23

Storm bowed hastily, then raced to the veranda, skidding on the bamboo-boarded path as she turned to fling herself in at Waffa's door. Then she stood stock-still in amazement.

Mer sat in one corner of the small single-roomed house. Her sleeping mat had been neatly folded and she sat upon it cross-legged. She glanced up briefly as Storm entered, then returned her gaze to her mother, who seemed deeply asleep. Waffa lay on a pallet beneath the single window, the shutters of which had been thrown wide to let in light and air.

The Bellum girl was not restrained in any way. No shackles or ropes. She could, Storm realised, have taken her sleeping mat and smothered her mother as she slept. But she had not. Why?

One look at Mer was enough to see that the girl had experienced something that had shaken her to the core. Storm took a hesitant step forward. She tried to sense Mer's thoughts and emotions. Her talent for empathy had never been so important.

"She sleeps. Still." Mer's voice was a monotone. The only emotion seemed to be exhaustion. Where was the hatred? The rage? Most of all, where was Mer's undying belief that she was in the right?

"Linnet says she will live."

"So it seems." Mer sighed. "Look at her. At her face. It might be carved from stone. How can she look so … normal? I have never been able to understand her. To read her. I have never been able to…"

"Love her?"

Mer met her eyes. "How can you love someone who does not love you back? Especially when that person is your own mother?"

Storm bit her lip. She doubted Waffa had ever loved anyone besides herself. "I'm sorry. We cannot choose our parents." She hesitated. One careless word might turn everything sour. "Your father loved you."

Amazingly, Mer did not explode. "Yes. I miss him so much! Every single day." Mer nodded at her sleeping mother and said, softy and sadly, "Killing her won't bring him back."

"Would her death make you happy?"

"I'm not even sure of that any more. I don't think I care what happens to her now."

"That's very different. What happened to change your mind?"

"The Dolphin happened." Mer gave a weary smile at Storm's astonishment. "Oh yes, I believe in the Elemental spirits now. How I could not? When one of them took the time to explain the error of my ways?"

"The Dolphin ... spoke to you?"

"Up close and *very* personal."

"But that means…"

"It means, Storm, that I have had my own unique Choosing ceremony. At the advanced age of sixteen years! Yes. The Dolphin spoke to me. It's a conversation I won't forget."

"So you're a Child of Water."

"I find I'm actually pleased." Mer grinned, somewhat ruefully. "I know I told you that we who are born into the Fifteen Families of the Pact are too sophisticated and important to believe in things like Elementals. The children of the Fifteen don't even have a Choosing Day! Well –" she sighed – "I've always loved sailing. Other than my father, being on the sea has been the one good thing in my life. So yes, I am happy to be a Child of Water. But now—" Mer broke off and gazed at Storm.

This was a new Mer. Uncertain, out of her depth.

"Who the Ancestors *am* I? What do I do now? Everything I thought I knew is … was … just not true! A fantasy. It was stuff I made up to justify what I wanted to do. And now? I don't know who I am, Storm. But –" Mer tossed her head, with a hint of her old ruthlessness – "I am going to be somebody! I'm going to make my father's spirit proud of me!"

"I think I might know how you could do that," said Storm.

Mer smiled a slow, considering smile. "I always knew I liked you, Storm of Yanlin. Please, do tell me."

←———→

"I don't believe it!" Nim sat on the edge of the veranda beside Storm. He stared open-mouthed at Linnet. "Mer? A change of heart? A shame she couldn't have had it before she tried to bash my brains out with an oar!" He rubbed the back of his head.

Nim had just returned from his mission in town and had much to tell them, but he eagerly accepted a bowl of rice and vegetables from Linnet. "This is so good!" He gobbled the first few mouthfuls, a look of rapture on his face. "I love rice! I love vegetables!"

"I remember," Storm said. "And you hate seaweed."

"With a passion!" He grinned at her.

"What news from our colleagues?" Linnet asked, when Nim finished eating.

"Mer's rebels have been harrying the Pact, disrupting the markets, recruiting Islanders. The place is like a rice pot overfilled and about to explode!"

"And the other witches?" asked Linnet. "What news from them?"

"Zephyr and Fountain, the two witches who helped rescue Storm, are still missing. If Mer really has changed her tune, then she must tell her people to release them. The town is crawling with witches. Some of them are performing magic tricks to earn enough to buy food and lodgings while waiting for the war to start."

"War?" Storm turned to Linnet. "But I thought we had stopped that."

"The Salamander fights on more than one front," Linnet replied. "The Elemental has sent every Fire-witch it can muster to Bellum. If the Drowned Ones fail to attack, it plans to set the island ablaze and kill as many as it can."

A chill tickled Storm's spine. "That's why the other witches are here. But they've been gathering all year.

How did you guess this part of the Salamander's plan?"

"There is not much the Tortoise does not know," Linnet said with a quiet smile. "Where there is land, earth or stone, it has knowledge. We have been expecting this and planning for it. But I will not pretend that I am not vastly relieved that you and Nim are back in time to help our side. The battle between the witches is, I fear, inevitable. It will be fierce."

"You won't be fighting alone," said a voice behind them.

Storm swung round to see Mer emerge from the shade of the veranda. "I've heard enough," said the Bellumer. "I will order my people to release your witch friends at once. And we'll help any way we can. No gassy ball of hot air is going to destroy my island! I'll make the Salamander regret the day it was born … I mean, created!"

Nim gave a shout of laughter. Mer scowled, then she gave a wry laugh. "Yes. Well. I've got a lot to learn about the Elementals. I guess they were created, which was a stupid thing to do if you ask me."

Now Linnet began to chuckle. Soon even Mer joined in. Storm laughed with delight, surprised by a moment of pure happiness. Life was best when you shared it with others. But life was fragile, like the wings of the butterflies dancing in Linnet's garden. Would she see these three all laugh together again?

24

"But why involve the Pact?" Mer asked for the fifth time. "Can't we settle this magic war first, *then* figure out how to take on the Pact? Fighting everyone at once means our forces will be diluted and we are more likely to lose!"

Linnet nodded, listening intently, as he had the previous four times. "I understand your concern, but we don't have time on our side. Bellum Town is a warren of hiding places. It would be impossible to track down all the Fire-witches quickly enough."

"How many of them are there?" Nim asked.

"I don't know." Linnet replied. "Perhaps twenty. Maybe fewer than ten. Not all have answered the Salamander's call. Some have rebelled and had their magic taken back by the Elemental."

He turned back to Mer. "Child, I fear we have no choice. Bellum needs to be secure before the Drowned Ones attack. The Tortoise tells me Rekka is with them, and that the Fire-witch has recovered much of her power. Of course, she might encourage the Drowned Ones to turn their attentions somewhere else first. Although I cannot imagine any other place where they could do as much damage."

"Damage." Storm murmured the word under her breath. Images flooded her mind's eye: Rekka, the abandoned child; Mer, overturning the canoe; Waffa floating, outlined in the Dolphin's light; her own mother, smiling at her.

"What is it?" Linnet asked, his eyes searching her face.

"You said that if Mer killed Waffa, the Salamander would gain a lot of strength. Why?"

Mer hunched her shoulders uncomfortably, but listened.

"Matricide kills more than the individual," Linnet said simply. "Pardon me, Mer, but Storm raises an important point. The amount of hatred that a person must hold in their hearts to kill the one who gave them life is … incalculable. And then, it is an attack on the process of life-giving itself. So, yes, a case of matricide would give the Salamander great power."

"Tell us what you're thinking, Storm," said Nim.

Storm's heart thudded. "If Rekka and the Drowned Ones decide not to attack Bellum, then I think I know where they will strike instead. The Fire-witch told me. She intends to kill her mother."

"Her mother lives?" Linnet asked. "Where?"

"I don't know if she's still alive. And it's not just her mother. Her father too. But it's worse than killing her parents…"

"Go on!" urged Nim.

"Rekka was cast out as a child. As a Seven-year."

"But that is monstrous!" Linnet exclaimed. "Why would an island do such a thing?"

"She said that her island's seer had predicted that Rekka was too dangerous to be allowed to live. That she would break the Balance some day. It seems that her Elders voted to cast her away on a uninhabitable speck of rock rather than kill her themselves."

"Blood-guilt," said Linnet. "Yes, they would have wanted to avoid that."

"There's more," Storm said reluctantly. "She … she intends to wipe out everyone living on her birth island in retribution. Possibly sink it beneath the sea, with the

Salamander's help. It's all she's dreamed of since that time."

"But if she was cast away on an uninhabitable rock, how did she survive?" Mer asked.

Storm remembered the story Rekka had told her – of walking across the sea over a bridge of burning lava – and shuddered. "The Salamander."

"Of course," Linnet said softly. "The seer was right. The Fire Elemental must have picked her early as its agent of destruction. Possibly before she was born. As the other Elementals Chose you."

Storm nodded. She was Rekka's twin in so many ways. When she looked up and caught Linnet gazing at her, Storm realised that the Earth-witch already knew that she, like Rekka, was a Child of Fire.

"I can't help but feel …" she said, "that I could have been like her."

"No, Storm. You think so because of the very thing that makes you unlike her: your imagination, your compassion. You tell yourself her story, and you feel it as if it was yours. You feel sorry for her … or for the child she once was. But that does not make you in any way similar to Rekka. The Tortoise, Albatross and Dolphin Chose you because you are *not* so." He sighed. "Your parents were good people. I do not know

Rekka's parents, but I cannot feel they loved her as they should."

"They should have fought for her! Or died with her," said Mer.

"We all make choices." Nim said. "Rekka chose her path. I almost took the wrong one." He looked at the Bellumer. "I'm pleased you decided, in the end, to travel with us."

Mer blushed. Storm couldn't tell if she was pleased, angry or merely embarrassed. The older girl turned to her. "So where is the Fire-witch's birth island?"

The three others looked expectantly at Storm. She shook her head. "That's just it. I don't know."

Linnet frowned. "In that case, we'll just have to hope news of the Drowned Ones' whereabouts reaches us before they attack Rekka's island."

"You mean news of raids on other islands along the way?" Nim asked.

Linnet nodded. "That is likely. Peggot will not turn away a chance to attack Islanders. So we must act quickly to secure Bellum from the Salamander and be ready when the news comes."

"And how are we going to secure Bellum?" Mer asked sceptically.

"We set a trap, child," said the Earth-witch. "We will

arrange a public meeting with Talon. I will make sure every Fire-witch in town knows the time and location of the meeting and hope both parties take the bait."

"And what bait would that be?" Mer asked.

"You, my dear."

←—————→

"The Pact will never, ever believe this," Mer grumbled as she and Storm navigated the twisting streets of Bellum Town, making for the central square. It was already swelteringly hot. "Or if they do, Talon will just have them shoot me on the spot." The Bellum rebel fidgeted with her mask. "I can't breathe in this stupid thing anyway!"

Mer's rebels had released the two witches they held as hostage and supplied their leader with a new black mask and robes embroidered with a ghostly narwhal. She looked every inch the dangerous rebel, but Storm felt the other girl's heart wasn't quite in it today.

"Talon won't have you shot immediately," she comforted Mer. "He'll want to know about Waffa's whereabouts. Besides, he'll want to humiliate you first."

"Oh, that's a great relief!" Mer snapped. "It's all right for you. You're used to witches trying to kill you."

"Linnet and Nim won't let us down. They and the

other witches should be more than a match for a dozen Fire-witches."

"Should be?"

"It'll be fine. I promise."

"Huh. I just feel better with a weapon in my hands."

"You have me, Mer."

The older girl darted a look at Storm, then nodded. "Thank you." The words came grudgingly but they came, and unaccountably lifted Storm's heart.

"We're nearly there," Mer said.

"I recognise it." They had just turned off one of Bellum Town's twisting side allies and emerged through an archway into the main square of the city.

"What if Talon didn't get the message?"

"Your people and Linnet's witches have been spreading the news in every square, tea shop and inn in town that you and I are going to demand a meeting with the Pact today. The Pact's spies are everywhere. By now both Talon and the Fire-witches know exactly where we are going to be at midday." Storm squinted overhead.

The sun glared from a white sky. Midday heat had turned the paved streets of Bellum Town into a bakehouse. Storm's heart began to speed up as the tingle of pre-battle nerves ran through her blood. Mer could be right: Talon might decide to shoot first and ask questions later. And no one knew how many of the Salamander's Fire-witches had gathered in Bellum over the past months.

The tall, expensive houses lining the square had their doors shut and shutters drawn. The square itself was nearly empty of stallholders and there was no sign of the swarms of town folk and visitors who normally crowded the marketplace.

The last three stallholders were striking their tents as Storm entered the square. One of the men spotted them, gave a tiny shriek of alarm, gathered an armful of bundles waiting on the ground and staggered off beneath them, abandoning his half-dismantled stall. The other two took one look and redoubled their efforts, heads averted, fingers fumbling with fear.

"Well," Mer said, "it looks like we're expected."

An imposing gatehouse led to the private area of the city claimed by the elite Pact. By the time they were standing in front of the enormous iron-clad door, the square had emptied, the last stallholder vanished, and any spectators who might have come along to witness the spectacle were hidden from sight. There was no sign of the guards who normally stood either side of the gate, waiting to interrogate and search all who wished to pass through into the Pact quarter.

"Looks like they don't want visitors today," Mer said.

"That's a shame," Storm said, trying to copy Mer's jaunty tone. They were both scared. The hairs on the back of her neck were prickling. Fire-witches would be watching her right now. Waiting for the right moment to attack. "Let's let them know we're here," she said. "Stand out of range in case there are archers waiting inside."

Mer stepped back. Storm gathered Air magic, waiting until she could feel an itchy pressure pushing in her head. She steadied her aim – precise magic was needed – then loosed a blast of compressed air right at the wooden door. It started at the back of the square, whooshed past them, making their tunics flap madly, and crashed into the wooden door, breaking two of the iron bands holding it to its hinges and leaving the door hanging drunkenly on a single hinge.

The ground-floor chamber of the guard house was empty, but she heard movement overhead and looked up, expecting to see archers bristling with arrows taking aim from the parapet. Instead, she saw a white flag waving frantically in the hands of a lone guard. "Parley!" the woman cried. "The Pact wishes to speak to Storm, the Weather-witch of Yanlin, and promises safe passage for her and her companion."

"Talon will have to speak to us in the public square," Storm replied. "We're not such fools as to walk into a trap. His word is useless, as he well knows. And if he is curious about what happened to Waffa, his tally-keeper, my friend here can tell him!"

25

The guard popped back out of sight like a rabbit into its hole. Storm glanced at Mer, who said, "He won't agree!"

"Perhaps," said Storm. "But he will be scared that Waffa is coming back to try for leadership of the Pact again. He will want to know her fate. Let's move into the middle of the square and wait."

"And become tempting bait for Fire-witches, is it?"

"That's the idea." Storm gave her companion a brief smile, but heart was pounding. Their footsteps echoed in the empty square as they walked slowly back to take up position facing the tower. What if Talon was cleverer than they thought and had set up an attacking force in the town? She readied her magic. The back of her neck crawled, and sweat beaded on her forehead and trickled down her face.

The silence deepened. Storm licked her lips. Mer swore under her breath and adjusted her mask. A figure emerged from the shadows beyond the broken door of the Pact's gatehouse. It was Talon, the Pact's leader.

Storm was surprised to see him emerge first. But a guard of a dozen archers and swords-folk immediately followed him out of the door. They stood beside and behind their leader – a semicircle bristling with iron.

The man who had tried to bribe her to become the Pact's own personal weapon against other islands had changed little. He still wore his fingernails long and painted with enamel. Today they were the same sea-green as his silk slippers, whose long pointed toes had to be tied to garters at his knees so he would not trip over them. Talon swanked across the sun-baked paving towards them, orange robes swishing, purple tricorn hat flapping. But, as he drew nearer, Storm saw that the band of his hat was sweat-stained, and his white face paint streaked. Even the kohl lining Talon's eyes had started to run in the heat, making him look like a startled tree-gibbon.

Storm waited, motionless, until the Pact leader swished to a halt a few paces from her and bowed with practised condescension. "Storm! It is so pleasant of you to grace our miserable island with your illustrious presence."

She bowed very slightly but kept her silence. The archers had advanced with their lord and now stood nearby, arrows notched but pointed to the ground. They could not miss at this distance. The swords-folk kept loosening their weapons in their scabbards. The message was clear.

Talon raised an eyebrow at her continued silence. "And what brings you back to Bellum?" He glanced from her to Mer. "And who might this extraordinarily costumed person be?"

"As of today, the Pact is no longer running Bellum Island." Storm tried to sound like Nim at his most confident. "The people will elect Elders, as is the ancient custom of the Islands, and it is they who will rule, with the consent of the ordinary folk of this island."

Talon stared at her incredulously, then tilted back his head and gave a mighty guffaw.

Good effort, said Storm's mind-voice. *But he's rattled. And as dangerous as a frightened snake.*

"You are a powerful witch, true." Talon whipped out an enormous yellow handkerchief and mopped delicately at his brow, then wiped his hands before tucking the cloth back in his waist pouch.

Buying time, observed Storm's mind-voice.

"However –" the Pact leader's voice was laced with acid – "you are only one witch, and even you can die if you should be unfortunate enough to be stuck full of arrows or get your head split open with a sword. So, considering the odds against you, I don't think even the Weather-witch of Yanlin can enforce her will on the Pact."

"You are making the mistake of thinking that I act alone."

"Hmmm." Talon flicked sea-green nails in the direction of Mer. "So *this* is your companion in this attempt at overthrow of the legitimate government of our island? One little girl in a pirate's costume?"

"Not quite," said Mer, and removed her mask. "I have a lot of friends. You may have heard of the Rebellion."

Talon's mouth dropped open. A flush rose from the high collar of his tunic to the stained rim of his tricorn hat, turning his painted face the orange-white of rotten salmon.

"You miserable little class-traitor!" he hissed. Then his eyes narrowed. "News of Waffa, eh? And what news do you have of your dear mother, Mer? Have you murdered her?"

Before Mer could answer, the shadow of an enormous bird blocked the sun's glare. Storm looked up to see the Albatross circling. The battle was upon them!

"It's time," she said to Mer.

"Got it!" Mer muttered, all jauntiness gone.

Storm and Linnet had discussed strategy long into the night. Now she set about creating a whirlwind. She would set it spinning around them to deflect hostile magic. She couldn't afford error. Talon must be inside the cyclone, his guards on the outside. Precise magic indeed!

Storm began to hum the Air music that had flooded her mind at the first sight of the Albatross. She sang louder and reached up to take even more magic from the sky. A gust of wind racketed around the square, huffing and blowing rubbish before it.

"What is going on?" Talon shouted.

"Just a few witches who want to kill us." Mer pointed. The Pact leader whirled round to see a dozen or more figures dart from the shadowy maze of side streets and alleyways leading on to the square and run towards them. The Fire-witches chanted as they advanced – a clanging brazen tune. Their arms and hands jerked and flicked as they gestured, preparing their attacks as they ran. Storm's skin prickled with the sheer amount of magic being activated in a confined space.

"A trick! A trick!" bellowed Talon. "Kill all the witches! All of them. Her first!" He pointed at Storm, who was too busy releasing her whirlwind to speak. She had no magic left to protect herself.

"No!" Mer whipped her poniard from its sleeve scabbard and held the point to Talon's throat. "Kill Storm and your master dies!"

The archers and swords-folk froze. They looked at each other, uncertain.

"Do as she says! Don't attack!" wheezed Talon, eyes wide with terror.

Storm barely noticed all this as she grunted with a final fierce effort and unleashed her magic. The sky darkened in the blink of an eye. The lonely trees scattered about the square groaned as their branches began to whip back and forth. Leaves and scraps of rubbish from the stalls raced and rattled as they were swept in furious circles over the paving stones.

Pressure built in the air inside the square until Storm's ears popped in protest. Tiles flew off several rooftops, sucked high into the air only to fall with even greater force, smashing to the ground. Storm heard a grunt, as one of Talon's guards was struck and fell like a dead thing.

There was a moment's eerie silence, then with a sucking, whistling roar, a whirlwind dropped from the sky, encircling the three of them. Mer screamed. Talon shrieked. Some of the archers shot arrows wildly. The rest of Talon's guard scattered, racing for the gatehouse as a dark wall of wind and accumulated rubbish swept around their lord, nearly obscuring him, the witch and the rebel from view. Storm, Mer and a sweating, wild-eyed Talon stood in the eye of a tornado.

Storm kept singing. Sweat dripped down her forehead and tickled her nose, but she didn't dare wipe it away. This was so much harder than she had expected. She had to control this revolving wall of furious wind, to keep it in one place, keep it spinning, feed it just enough energy.

Inside the howling wall of wind, Talon and Mer seemed frozen in awe, barely flinching as fireballs were launched towards them by the Salamander's witches, who were now struggling to stay on their feet and avoid being sucked into the whirlwind. One after the other, the fireballs shot forward only to be deflected by the force of the cyclone and spun off sideways or back towards the witches themselves.

"What is all this about?" Talon had discovered his voice.

"We're saving Bellum Island," Mer answered.

Storm hardly listened. She doubled down on her concentration; she was starting to tire. Where were Nim and the other witches? Surely it was time for them to come to their aid and ambush the ambushers?

"Waffa sold you out," Mer told Talon. "She was working with the Drowned Ones. They planned to use Bellum as a base to take over all the islands. I stopped her. Well … Storm and I did. But now we have an even bigger problem to sort out, and these Fire-witches are not a good thing!"

"I guessed that." Talon's voice was acid.

"Then be quiet and do as you're told, and you might live to tell this tale to your grandchildren. That is if you can convince anyone to marry your monster of a daughter!"

"Get ready to run for cover!" Storm gasped. "I can't hold on any more." She could feel the whirlwind falter, the force stutter. She was at the end of both concentration and strength.

"Blast! Where's Nim?" Mer grabbed Talon by the front of his tunic. "You're coming with me. Try anything and I'll gut you like a carp!"

Storm released her magic and dropped to one knee, panting. The whirlwind vanished with a scream like that of a disappointed ghost, leaving behind a wind-scoured ring on the pavement and exposing Storm to her enemies.

The looks on the faces of the dozen or so Fire-witches gathered in the square changed from fear and frustration to surprise and then glee.

The flow of expressions would have been funny in other circumstances, Storm thought as she knelt and dug deep into her reserves of strength. She had to try to defend against the coming strikes. Of course it was hopeless: she might fight off one or two at most. Still, she would go down fighting, as Ma had done.

Scuffling footsteps and muttered swearing retreated behind her as Mer dragged Talon out of the strike zone. Storm was on her own – target practice for a swarm of angry Fire-witches. Her mind automatically registered the witch who would attack first. As the man raised his hand to strike, Storm rolled sideways, lunged to her feet and blasted him with a gust of wind. The Fire-witch went flying. Storm was already running.

Three figures darted to cut her off. She skidded to a stop, dodged left. It was no use: the Salamander's agents were converging on her from all sides. A man ran towards her. He tossed a fireball, hate and fear melting his face into an ugly mask. Storm ducked and the missile passed harmlessly overhead. With a gasp, she flung a fistful of wind at the nearest witch just as the woman shot a fireball from her outstretched fingers. The two missiles met mid-air with a loud bang and explosion of sparks.

A man darted into sight on Storm's left. "Try that with this one!" he shouted.

She whirled, gathering the last of her magic, knowing she couldn't save herself this time. The Fire-witch's arm shot up, fingers already glowing red. But before he could launch his attack, a deafening crack echoed around the square, and the pavement where he was standing split apart. With a yelp of alarm, the witch dropped waist deep in the fissure. Then he screamed as the earth closed up again, catching him like a mouse in a trap.

Storm stared in amazement as another Fire-witch was swallowed up to her chest in earth. Both of them writhed frantically, unable to escape the earth's grip. The remaining two Fire-witches closest to Storm were lifted off their feet by a sudden blast of wind and sent sprawling before they could complete their attacks on her.

Storm heard the trill of a flute rise above the din of battle. That was Zephyr, the Air-witch! Then she heard a familiar voice singing Earth magic. Nim and the other witches had arrived at last!

Storm felt a new flush of strength. She began singing, joining in with Nim. Zephyr's flute trilled and she was lifted up on a wave of power. With their aid, she rose into the air on a spinning whirlwind and began to sweep down the square, herding the last of the panicking Fire-witches towards Nim and Mer's rebel soldiers. One by one, the Fire-witches were subdued, bound and led away.

When the last enemy was vanquished, Storm let go of the music of Air and flopped to the ground with a shout of relief. She lay back, exhausted and exhilarated in equal measure, and stared up at the sky. The storm clouds had melted away. Overhead, an enormous Albatross circled slowly on the thermals before drifting higher and higher until it faded from sight.

26

A very different Talon stood before the crowd assembled
to watch his trial. The Pact leader's purple tricorn hat
had been lost in the scuffle. His slippers were scuffed
and torn. The long, pointed toes dragged in the dirt,
threatening to trip him whenever he moved. His white
face paint was blotchy and streaked with sweat, and he
smelled of fear. But still, Storm noticed, Talon clung to
the tatters of his dignity. He held his head up, pretending
unconcern. She was impressed despite herself. To be
afraid and still behave well was admirable, even in a
rogue like Talon.

"I am not, obviously," Talon said, "in a position
to argue the legality, or indeed the merits, of your
demands. But I refuse – I absolutely refuse – to be tried
and condemned alongside that ... that traitor!" He

pointed to Waffa, who sat hunched on a rug, huddled in a cloak even though the day was hot.

They stood upon a wooden platform that had been hastily erected to give a view of the proceedings to the citizens of the city. Ropes were strung in a giant web from the roofs of buildings surrounding the central square of Bellum Town. The web had been roofed with palm leaves, forming an open-sided tent where the people of the town could shelter from the sun while attending the first town meeting in generations. The square was crowded with the Bellumers who had just elected Elders for the first time in their lives.

"Would you prefer to be executed alongside her without a hearing?" Mer asked.

Talon's brave front collapsed at once. "Execute? You can't possibly… I have done nothing wrong!"

"I was just pulling your leg." Mer smiled nastily. "Maybe."

Linnet, standing beside Mer as Talon's joint accuser, put a warning hand on the rebel leader's arm. "No one is going to be executed," said the Earth-witch, who had just been appointed chief Elder. "We are now handing over proceedings to our new Council of Elders. As is tradition among all Islanders, we will hear the evidence and pronounce judgement.

"If you and the other Pact members are found guilty of usurping the power of the people and stealing the wealth of the island for your personal use, then the Elders will sentence each of you. But there will be no executions. We will not feed the Salamander further at a time when the Balance of All Things teeters on the edge of destruction."

Storm and Nim stood in the middle of the watching crowd. She glanced at Nim. The Drowned One was frowning thoughtfully. As if he felt her gaze, he turned to her with a quizzical smile. "They don't look happy, do they?" He nodded towards the heads of the Fifteen Pact Houses, who had been rounded up by Mer's rebels and stood huddled together at the back of the platform. "Do you think Linnet will be able to control Mer? I think she'd still rather solve her arguments with sharp iron rather than words."

"She's changed. The Dolphin changed her. As did you."

"Me?" Nim raised his eyebrows. "What did I do?"

"You saved her life. Peggot would have killed her – we both know that. Mer knows it too."

At the mention of his tribe's Elder, Nim's face went wooden.

"I'm sorry," Storm said. She knew what it meant to

feel an outsider, but even at her loneliest she had always had Ma and Minnow. Nim was totally alone.

"It will always hurt." He took a deep breath, shrugged. "But I'm still alive and so is my dream of a better life for my people. Peggot and her kind won't be around forever."

"Being young doesn't mean you're any less bloodthirsty. Look at Mer. And she's not the only one."

Something in her voice made Nim turn to study her. "Who do you mean?"

"I just had a message from my island."

"Yanlin?"

"The islands in the Outer Sea sent a delegation to Bellum. It arrived yesterday. We need to talk to Linnet. Urgently."

←———→

The sun had transformed into a plump orange ball floating above the horizon by the time Storm managed to gather Linnet, Mer and Nim in one place. Dusk brought a welcome coolness to the air blowing off the sea.

All fifteen Pact leaders had been convicted of corruption and their houses and goods seized. They were not imprisoned, but each would have to work as general labourers in the town, and live in a communal building where they would report each day to an Elder. Their expensive homes were to be turned into schools to train apprentices. This, the Elders hoped, would in time ensure that Bellum Island would once more become an island of Makers. Waffa had been given into the care of the local healer until she was fit to stand trial.

"Which will be never," Mer said coldly. "She's lost her mind."

Storm saw emotion after emotion cross the older girl's face. It would take Mer a long time to heal too. If time was granted to any of them. She turned her attention to Linnet's discussion with her uncle, Lake, whose ship, the *Wayfarer*, had sailed into Bellum harbour with the news she had been both fearing and hoping for.

"Captain Lake," said Linnet. "I'm sorry you've had to wait so long after your journey before speaking to the Elders of Bellum, but please tell us your news."

"The wait was worth it!" said Lake. "I had little hope of help from Talon or the Pact, but things have changed here at last, and not before time!"

"Thanks to your niece." Linnet bowed to Storm.

"Thanks to the Ancestors for saving her life!" Lake's own face grew red with emotion. "The whole of Yanlin has been in mourning, believing you dead, Niece. Only

Minnow believed you would survive. He said his bees told him so!"

"I have learned to believe everything Minnow says about his bees," Storm said with a smile. She longed to hear about home and her young cousin, but this wasn't the time. "You bring important news, Uncle. News we had expected and feared."

"Do you have information about the Fire-witch, Captain Lake?" asked Linnet.

"There are reports of raiding by Drowned Ones." Nim's voice was harsh, his face hard a stone. "Rekka will be with them. They are in the Outer Sea, then?"

Lake frowned, studying Nim as if trying to place him. To Storm's relief he gave up and nodded. "The boy is right. Island after island has been attacked. The pirates are travelling south from the Inner Sea. It's bad. I've never heard of such a string of attacks – or such devastation! The rumour is that the Drowned Ones have a tame Fire-witch! They're attacking island after island. But…" Lake shook his head. "No one can figure it out."

"Figure what out, Uncle?"

"They attack, kill, plunder and then leave. Not one island has been stolen, It's like they don't want islands any more!"

"Rekka's home island." Storm met Linnet's gaze. "It's in the Outer Sea. It must be! She must be bribing Peggot and the Drowned Ones to take her there by helping them plunder every island in easy reach along the way."

"The Fire-witch?" Lake shook his head. "I don't know anything about where her home island is, or why she wants to go there. But I do know that the Drowned Ones scum have to be stopped before they attack every island in the Outer Sea. People are dying! And…"

For the first time in her life, Storm saw her uncle look confused and unsure. Lake always knew what he thought about things.

"Since the Drowned Ones' attacks began, there have been new volcanic eruptions in the Outer Sea. They follow the reef that runs east of the archipelago. There are more eruptions every day. Cones are pushing above the water line; magma is pouring out. The sky over the reef is filled with smoke. It drifts as far south as Yanlin. The Outer Sea is on fire!"

27

"Thank you for coming to warn us." Linnet looked grave. "The hunt begins, Storm. We must track down the Fire-witch and put an end to this before the Salamander gains too much power. The Drowned Ones are definitely heading for Rekka's home island. Its destruction will give Fire enough power to break the Balance once and for all!"

"A moment, Elder Linnet." Storm bowed in apology for interrupting the old Earth-witch. "There's more to this. Uncle, you said you wanted Bellum's help. What help? You couldn't have known about the Fire-witch or the Salamander's plans."

"The Salamander?" Lake stared at his niece in horror. "Elder Teanu has been talking about the Balance being in danger. I must admit, I gave her little heed. She's been talking of little else since you disappeared … and the Drowned One attacks… At least you can fight the pirates. You can't fight an Elemental spirit!"

Storm sighed. Lake was a good man, but he lacked imagination. "Please, Uncle, tell us what help you wanted from the Pact? What are the islands in the Outer Sea planning?"

"We want Bellum's harrier ships."

"Why?" Nim barked. His eyes sparked like iron-struck flint.

Lake frowned. Storm could see her uncle was offended by Nim's abruptness. But he kept his temper as he answered. "To get rid of the cursed pirates, of course. We've been petitioning every island from the Outer to the Inner Sea. We're gathering every trading vessel and fishing boat that can be spared in order to form a war fleet. We will attack and destroy the pirate scum's raft towns. And this time we'll put a permanent end to their marauding. We'll defeat them, then hunt the survivors down to the last raft and canoe. Not one of the stinking rats will be left alive!"

"I'm one of those stinking rats!" Nim growled.

Storm put a hand on his arm. "I apologise for my uncle."

Nim's face had gone very pale. Now his colour

returned. He nodded and stepped back. But he stared at Lake, and his gaze was bitter.

"A Drowned One? This isn't… By the Ancestors, Storm!" Lake lurched forward, his hand reaching for his belt knife. Before he could launch himself at Nim, Mer drew her own and presented its point to Lake's nose.

"You won't do anything stupid, I'm sure, Captain Lake," she purred. "I'd hate to have to hurt you, but Nim is my friend."

"Friend be cursed! He's a Drowned One! He's the pirate brat who hid himself on Yanlin. He tricked you, Storm! He betrayed you and my son and caused your mother's death. Dain died because of that … that animal! And you stand there, protecting him?"

"Nim is also my friend, Uncle." Storm took Nim's hand in hers. "He has saved my life several times now. Also, his tribe has disowned him."

"I'm still a Drowned One!" Nim said, his words uneven, his breathing ragged as he struggled for control. "I will be a Drowned One to the end of my days! My people are as human as you, old man! If you Land Grubs had ever thought to help us, to share your good fortune, our peoples would not be at war."

"And if you pirates had ever asked instead of

raising our islands—"

"Enough!" shouted Linnet.

Storm jumped. She had never heard the old Earth-witch raise his voice before.

"This war between Islanders and Drowned Ones must cease," Linnet continued, "or there will be no one left alive to argue on either side! Bellum's harriers will not join in a war against the Drowned Ones."

"But—"

"Don't fret, Captain," Mer said. "Bellum's harriers *will* sail tomorrow! I will lead them myself in the *Narwhal*. But we will not make war on the Drowned Ones. We go in search of Peggot's raft town and the Fire-witch."

Linnet nodded. "Storm and Nim must go with you."

"Absolutely. I might manage Peggot and her warriors, but not Rekka." Mer shuddered. She turned to Lake, who was staring opened-mouthed at them, utterly confused. "I will explain, Captain. Bellum against the other islands; Islanders against Drowned Ones. We humans simply can't afford to battle among ourselves any longer, or there will be no life – human or otherwise – left on land or in sea." She caught Storm's eye and shrugged. "Don't smirk at me: the Dolphin is very convincing!"

Nim shook his head doubtfully. "You're gambling on the Bellum harriers being able to prevent the Islanders from attacking the Drowned Ones. That's by no means a sure bet!"

"We should head to Yanlin first of all," Storm said. "I will ask our fleet to help." She looked at her uncle. "You must help me convince them, Uncle. The Salamander's Fire-witch will not be defeated easily."

Lake scratched his head. It was plain that he was struggling to come to terms with what he had just learned. "Elementals? The Salamander and a Fire-witch? I don't know what to make of it all but you've never lied to me, Storm, and you've never let your island down. I'm with you, but it won't be easy to convince some folk on Yanlin. We must talk to Teanu. Perhaps she can manage Cloud."

Cloud, the boy who had once been Storm's friend. Cloud, who dreamed of revenge on the Drowned Ones. Who thought that being a hero meant you should kill your enemies rather than talk to them.

"Young Cloud hasn't been the same since the time in Bellum when we lost you," Lake said. "He used to be lazy, but the boy's turned into a proper firebrand. Never stops talking war. At it all day, training with sword and bow. Wants to lead the attack against the Drowned Ones himself." Lake shrugged. "The youngsters listen to him. To be honest, he had me half convinced that all our problems would be over if we killed off all the Drowned Ones! But the Balance comes before anything. Even killing pirates." Lake glared at Nim, who stared back stony-faced.

←⎯⎯⎯→

Supplies had been loaded on to the *Narwhal* and Mer waited impatiently on board to begin the journey to Yanlin. It was early morning, but the stones of Bellum's quay were already hot beneath her sandals as Storm watched Nim say goodbye to Linnet. Scoundrel had travelled down to the quay on the boy's shoulders, but now he leapt through the air and settled on the old Earth-witch, putting a long arm round the old man's neck and blinking at Nim and Storm from huge amber eyes.

"Scoundrel will wait here on Bellum Island until you return, Nim," said Linnet. "You must come back for him, for he is your companion now."

"I can't take him from you!" Nim protested.

"The Tortoise Chose Scoundrel to be his emissary, as he Chose the two of us to be his witches. Now my work for the Earth spirit is done, and it is time for me to rest. You are the Tortoise's Earth-witch now, Nim, and your work is just beginning. Scoundrel belongs with you."

"The Tortoise's Earth-witch!" For a heartbeat Nim looked appalled. Then the Drowned One boy bowed deeply to the old Earth-witch. "Then I will certainly need Scoundrel's help! Thank you, Linnet," he said, "for everything."

"Remember that you will always have a home here. A place to stay until you can return to your tribe when the time is right." He turned to Storm. "Fare thee well, child. The journey nears its end. Have faith in yourself, and return when you are able. I shall miss you!"

Storm smiled at him, her heart full. "Thank you for everything Linnet – I will remember your words." She bowed low, then joined Nim in the canoe waiting to ferry them to the *Narwhal*. Nim rowed and Storm sat in the bow, watching the figure of the old Earth-witch grow slowly smaller until he and the cling-monkey disappeared from view.

←——————→

Storm sat near the prow of the *Narwhal*, her hair streaming behind her. Automatically, her hand reached up to count the thirteen plaits again. Half a year ago, half a lifetime ago, she had sailed from Yanlin harbour, her hair cut short and tied in a topknot.

She had been made a non-sex, neither girl or boy,

because tradition said girls could not be Weather-witches and they must not sail with the fleet. Well, she was a girl *and* a Weather-witch, and anyone who didn't like it could tell her to her face.

Soon she would see the familiar seamarks that would tell her she was approaching her home. She had been able to swim before she could walk, to sail before she could run. The seas around Yanlin were as familiar as the paths of her village. She both longed and feared to set foot on her island again. To see Minnow, Aunt Briathe and Elder Teanu. Mixi, her old enemy … maybe a friend of the future? But…

Storm faced the wind, eyes half closed against the pain. Even now, more than a year later, grief was like a jagged knife plunged in her heart. The hurt never grew less, she just got used to living with it a little more each day. To go through the door of Dain's house – the home her mother had made for them both. To be in that house of memories, with Ma forever dead, resting in the Ancestor cave. She feared it more than the Fire-witch.

The wind blew her thirteen plaits behind her; it blew the tears from her face.

28

"How dare you!" Storm held her cousin's work-roughed hands and stood back to study his face. "You've grown as tall as me!"

Minnow grinned. "Get used to it, Cousin!" He swept her into a hug. She hugged back fiercely. If only Time could stop now, with the person she loved most safe in her arms. She kissed Minnow on the cheek and stepped back once more, continuing her inspection.

Her cousin's topknot was on the verge of tumbling down, so nothing had changed there. He wore gardening clothes, sun-faded and earth-stained. Minnow was as untidy as ever and looked happy, strong and healthy. His work as the island's chief gardener suited him.

"Huh. Well, you're getting enough to eat, from the looks of you. How are the pumpkins this year?"

"I always make sure to get enough to eat. And you'll sample my pumpkins at tonight's feast." Minnow grinned widely. "Do you have time to visit my bees? They told me you would come today."

"I'd love to. And I want to see your garden. And hear all your news. But I have to speak with Teanu first."

Minnow nodded, his face suddenly grave. "Something big is happening. The bees are worried. But you'll fix it, Storm. You and Nim." Her cousin turned to smile shyly at the Drowned One. "It's good to see you, Nim. You're an Earth-witch, aren't you?"

Nim's smile of welcome changed to a look of amazement. "How did you know that?"

Storm laughed. Nim's face was comic. "His bees told him, of course. Am I right?"

"Perhaps." Minnow's face wore a look of pride, intense and private.

"The Tortoise," Nim said. "It speaks to those who can listen. Like those bees of yours." He grinned. "It's good to see you, Minnow. How is your leg?"

"I'll never win a foot race, but it works fine." Minnow shrugged. Nim had saved him from a cloud leopard, but Storm's cousin would always limp. That was why the Elders had granted his wish to be a gardener, rather than making Minnow sail with the fleet like all the

226

other boys. "Look!" he pointed to the harbour, where a trading vessel was sailing slowly past the breakwater to anchor next to the *Narwhal*. "The *Wayfarer*! I'll go and greet my father, and then I must get back to helping with tonight's feast. See you later, Storm." He beamed at Nim and limped away towards the harbour.

Mer had gone ahead to meet the island Elders. Now she motioned for them to join the crowd of onlookers who had gathered as soon as the *Narwhal* drew in sight of Yanlin's harbour.

As Storm walked along the pier where she used to play with her friends, she saw Teanu and her heart smiled. Last year, she had been the same height as Yanlin's chief Elder. But when Storm finished her low bow of respect and stood straight again, she found she had to look down to meet Teanu's gaze. The old woman had never been tall, but her once straight back was hunched, and she clutched her Elder's cane for support. But Teanu's eyes still sparkled, and her long plaits fell shining from her head like a silver waterfall.

Storm's heart gave a pang as she saw that her mentor and friend had aged, in one of those sudden leaps towards mortality that ambush the very old. Teanu's voice, however, remained firm and clear: "Welcome, Storm of Yanlin. It is so good to have you home!

Come, I have ordered food and drink. We will meet with the Elders in the hut. There is much to discuss." Teanu turned to face Nim and her smile faded. "The Drowned One Earth-witch, I believe?"

Nim stiffened, unsure of his welcome. After all, he had helped his tribe invade Yanlin less than two years ago. Many Islanders had died.

Teanu inclined her head in a formal bow. "A *peace-loving* Earth-witch is welcome on Yanlin."

Nim nodded curtly. "My thanks."

Storm sighed. Peace between their tribes still seemed far away.

←——————→

Tea was served in small porcelain bowls glazed in shades of palest green. Storm took hers with a painful squeeze of the heart. Dain's work. She held the bowl of fragrant liquid in her fingertips, closed her eyes as she slurped the first delicious mouthful, and did her best to accept the pain and tea with equal grace. Ma would expect it. Dain's words rang in her head: *I believe that when you make something good and true you put a part of yourself inside it that stays there forever.*

"Some of your mother's finest work." Teanu was watching. "But you are her best. You will succeed."

Storm quickly bent her head for another sip. She was

grateful when Mer interrupted: "Have you Yanliners heard anything of the Drowned Ones' whereabouts?"

"They are headed this way," said Teanu. "We have news that Waysun Island was attacked last week."

"That's too close!" exclaimed an Elder. "They will be here within days." The room suddenly seemed hot and breathless with tension, even though the window was unshuttered and the smell of wixcaxi blossom wafted on the breeze.

Set in the warm belly of the town, the Elders' hut was the heart of Yanlin. The simple one-room building dominated the open space in the middle of the town where Islanders gathered to celebrate and to mourn. Storm's first visit to the hut had been just after her Choosing, when the Elders had found out that she was a witch. Now Mer and Nim had been invited to drink tea with the Elders to celebrate her return to Yanlin and discuss the threat that had brought her home.

The familiar room was crowded … and not just with Elders.

She was astonished to see Cloud lounging in a corner, scowling at Nim. Beside him stood Mixi, her old enemy. Mixi caught Storm's eye and gave a faint nod – not warm, but not hostile either. Their truce held. But what were she and Cloud doing here at all?

Only Elders and those they wished to question attended important meetings such as these.

Without invitation from the Elders, Cloud spoke: "The Islands of the Outer Sea are joining to finish the pirate scum off once and for all." He pointed at Mer. "You! Bellumer. My people say five Bellum harriers are anchored off Yanlin. I want them to join the hunt."

A shocked silence engulfed the hut. Storm stared at Cloud in disbelief. Why were the Elders allowing such impertinence from a boy hardly past Choosing?

Mer responded before the shocked Elders could speak. She raised an eyebrow and regarded Cloud, clothed in all her old Pact arrogance. "And who might you be? Not an *Elder* of Yanlin, I think."

"Cloud!" Teanu had struggled to her feet. Now she thumped her Elder staff on the boarded floor with much of her old force. "You have been given permission to attend the Elders' meeting only because you and your followers threatened to be disruptive if you were not allowed to do so. That is blackmail, and you will answer to us for that crime when dangers to our island are less pressing. Do not presume further on our patience! You are not here to speak but to listen!"

Cloud shrugged and returned to staring spitefully at Nim.

"I will, however, answer the boy's question," Mer said. "All of you need to know that Bellum's harriers will *not* help you fight the Drowned Ones."

At her words Elder Gol, the oldest of Yanlin's leaders, pushed herself to her feet and thumped her staff on the floor in protest. "Then why are you here, Bellumer? Why will you not help us? The Drowned Ones are a curse upon us all. They must be eliminated!"

Storm grabbed Nim's sleeve in warning. "May I speak?" she asked Teanu, who nodded permission.

Storm bowed to Gol. "Elder, know that you are not aware of all the facts. The Drowned Ones do not act alone. They are being used by the Salamander's agent, Rekka the Fire-witch, to bait us. It is a trap. We must on no account attack the Drowned Ones' fleet—"

"Traitor!" Cloud shouted, stepping forward to shake his fist at Storm.

All seven Elders stood – in a dusty confusion of creaking joints and huffing breath – and began thumping the floor with their staffs. The din was deafening. It drowned Cloud's shouting. It hammered away the last sense of peace in the hut. It even vanquished the smell of wixcaxi blossom.

Storm did not ask for permission this time. She marched round the flock of outraged Elders and advanced on Cloud. The staffs broke rhythm, faltered and stopped. The room was quiet when Storm reached her former friend. They stood, face to face, glare to glare. The small room, sticky with heat and the perfume of wixcaxi, fell so silent that Storm could hear her own breathing. And Cloud's.

"Did you go to the Ancestor caves and give my grave gift to Thorn?"

Cloud stared at her, dumbfounded. "Yes," he said, after a long silence. "But wh—"

"You should have stayed in the caves to listen to the wisdom of his spirit! Thorn was the best of us – all of us Thirteen-years who gathered to dive off the pier, to sit on the beach in the warm sand and swap stories. He knew true courage meant listening to just grievances. He knew it meant more than winning – that sometimes losing what you desire takes the greatest courage. Most of all, Thorn knew that it takes more bravery to admit that you are wrong than it does to kill someone to prove you are right. And I am no traitor!"

All the time she was talking, Cloud's face had grown redder, hotter. "What else should you be called? You bring him to Yanlin!" Cloud pointed at Nim. "The pirate scum that killed Thorn same as if he'd stuck him with his knife!"

Behind her, the Elders breathed and muttered like willows in a wind. Cloud's words had struck home with many. None of her people would forget the Drowned Ones' attack on Yanlin. Many, she knew, would never forgive. But she had to try to convince them.

"Many died on that day," Storm said. "Nim did what he felt was right for his tribe. He has been brave enough to admit he was wrong. He has apologised to me for his part in that day. Now he fights – not for the Drowned Ones, and not for the Islanders. He fights for the Balance of All Things. Without it there will be no Drowned One tribe, no Islander tribe! All will perish.

"Also, you should know that Nim is an Earth-witch and a powerful one. The Tortoise itself guides him!"

The room buzzed with surprised murmurs from the Elders. Storm ignored them and continued: "He is a hero who sacrificed his future with his people to fight the Salamander and keep the Balance!" Storm stood tall, and her heart was glad as she said, "He is also my friend."

"He is responsible for your own mother's death!" spat Cloud. "And you are too cowardly to put an end to his life. Well, I will be glad to do that job for you."

"You will not!" Storm said, sadness filling her heart. Cloud was lost. His heart was too full of himself to allow him to hear any other voice. "What you *will* do is leave this hut. You will wait, like all the rest of the people of our island, to be told the results of our meeting. That is our tradition; those are our laws. And then you will do as your Elders bid you."

"And if I don't?"

"Then you will answer to me." Their gazes locked. Storm remembered the boy who had been her companion on her first voyage as a Weather-witch. The boy who longed to be an Air-witch, hiding his jealousy even from himself. Only he misunderstood the strength he craved. Now, as she looked into his eyes, she saw anger become hatred and bitterness.

29

Cloud turned and walked from the hut. Mixi had stood silently all this time, a puzzled frown on her face. Storm saw her shoot a look of pure venom at Nim. Mixi had loved Dain too. But the other girl's eyes were confused and uncertain as she turned and left the hut.

The Elders waited. Some faces were pale with outrage, others dark with anger, some long with worry. Yanlin's Elders waited for her to speak. It was terrifying.

Storm took another deep breath. *Dain,* she prayed, *lend me your strength and wisdom. I shall need all of it.* She glanced at Mer and Nim. They gazed back gravely, waiting. She looked at Teanu. The Elder nodded her approval, and Storm's heart felt a shade less heavy.

"Come," said Teanu. "We have work to do."

"You are forbidden!" Teanu and the six other Elders stood on the town platform, expressing their outrage at Cloud, Mixi and a group of young, and not young, Yanliners.

"You cannot stop us." Cloud glanced round at his supporters, who responded to his words with shouts and cheers of encouragement. "You are too old to know what is best for Yanlin!"

Storm gasped. To live long enough to grow old was a gift granted to very few. Elders were precious, wise, valuable. Those Islanders who stood beside the Elders in support answered Cloud's words with shouts of outrage.

Teanu raised her hand and silence fell, except for muttering from Cloud's group of rebels. "And I say that whoever sails from this island in order to attack the Drowned Ones will not be able to return!"

Silence fell as the enormity of the words was understood by both sides of the argument. The best someone exiled from their island could hope for was a life as an itinerant trader, even a pirate. The worst was death, for other islands did not often take in those rejected by their own.

"This is our home too!" Cloud stormed. "When we have finished with the Drowned Ones we will return and reclaim it!"

"I will oppose you," Storm said. "Will you battle me, Cloud? Do you have courage enough for that? Perhaps you'd like to fight me now?"

The boy who had once been her shipmate shook with silenced fury. He turned and marched towards the harbour, shouting over his shoulder: "Those of you who want revenge on pirate scum follow me. The rest of you be cursed as cowards!"

Lake ran after his former apprentice. "You'll not touch the *Wayfarer*, young Cloud! Try to take my ship and I'll skin you alive!"

One by one, half of Cloud's followers, some two dozen young and older men, and even a few of the young women, marched after him towards the harbour, ignoring the pleas of wives, girlfriends and parents. The rest hung their heads and melted into the crowd.

Storm saw Mixi hesitate, then walk slowly to stand beside Minnow, who reached out and took her hand. Part of her was hurt by the sight, but more of her was glad. Minnow had forgiven Mixi for trying to kill him, and Storm could forgive her old enemy for loving Dain. Her mother had had enough love to share with all of them.

There had been no time, after all, to visit Minnow's bees. Storm stood in the bow of the *Narwhal* with the wind she had called whipping her braids in front of her face. Her cousin would forgive her. The bees would tell him everything he needed to know, until she could return to tell him herself. She could trust the Tortoise to look after his Children, especially one so precious and life-loving as Minnow. Even if she didn't return, her island would be safe in his work-hardened hands, and Teanu's wise and clever ones.

She's dying, said her mind-voice. *She will not see the monsoon rains return.* In her heart Storm knew it was true: Teanu was fading. But she pushed the thought from her mind.

"The *Narwhal* can take more, if you have it!" Mer called from the stern, where she held the rudder in experienced hands. Nim was below deck, fixing something to eat. Like many Earth-witches, he seemed to have a talent for cooking. Storm was acting as crew, obeying Mer's orders with pleasure. She loved being aboard ship, and Mer's sailing talent was mesmerising.

Nim popped out of the open hatch, holding a coconut half full of rice and vegetables in each hand as he negotiated the deck, ducking under the boom as it swayed towards him, leaping over coiled rope. He gave

Storm a shell full of steaming, delicious-smelling food, then went to the stern of the ship, moving with the ease of one born at sea. "Here you go, Captain." He took the rudder from Mer as she scooped the food up and began shovelling it into her mouth. "Yummm! This is gorgeous, Nim! I'm so hungry."

"Where's yours?" Storm asked. "Mer's right. This is the best!"

Nim grinned. "I ate mine already. Couldn't resist. Minnow's peas and sweetcorn are amazing. And as for his pumpkin? That boy can come and live with me when this is all over."

"You'll just have to come and live on Yanlin," Storm said, and cursed herself as she saw Nim's grin – something far too rare now – slip from his face. Of course he couldn't live on Yanlin. He would always be the Drowned One who helped his people stage a deadly attack.

"Sorry," she said.

He shrugged. "None of us will live anywhere if we don't beat your idiotic friend to Peggot and Rekka."

"Storm's uncle will lead him a merry dance." Mer sounded full of confidence. "It's a race. This is fun! We'll find your stinking raft town first, all right. My worry is what happens after that."

"We have a plan." Storm tried to sound just as confident. "Lake leads Cloud on a goose chase and your harriers keep the Drowned Ones occupied while we tackle Rekka."

"Lots can go wrong," Nim said. "Cloud might not fall for the bait. He might strike off on his own."

"If he does, Lake will stop him. The *Wayfarer* is bigger and faster than the ship Cloud and his rebels stole. And Lake is an experienced captain. Cloud isn't. Lake can sail rings round him. They'll board them if necessary!"

"Lake might defeat Cloud peacefully enough," Nim said, "but Peggot won't hold back if Mer's harriers go after her. There will be deaths. And that's just—"

"What we're trying to avoid. I know! Do you have a better plan?" Storm hadn't meant to snap, but hearing her own worries thrown back at her wasn't helpful.

Mer interrupted. "I haven't heard anything about how you two are going to tackle Rekka. I'd focus on that, if I were you, and stop arguing."

"I don't know how strong the Fire-witch is now," said Storm. "My only plan is to stop her killing her parents and destroying the island. Whatever it takes. And it will take Nim's help." She turned to him. "I need you with me."

"I'll be there," Nim said. "We'll finish this, one way

or the other."

Storm's mouth felt suddenly dry.

"More wind!" commanded Mer. "How many times do I have to ask, Storm? And you!" she shouted at Nim. "More food! Now!" Mer grinned as they turned in unison to glare at her. "That took your mind off it. You should see your faces," she said, and hooted with laughter.

"Over there!" Nim pointed.

"I don't see anything." Storm squinted at the horizon, but all she could see were endless whitecaps and a few cloud shadows playing hide-and-seek among the waves.

"There's nothing there," said Mer. "Your eyes are playing tricks, Nim."

"Trust me," he said. "It's a raft town. And beyond it, an island."

"If you say so." Mer adjusted the tiller, the boom swayed left and the *Narwhal* leapt like a dolphin to the right, climbing wave after wave. She had steered the *Narwhal* tirelessly all day without complaint, while Storm and Nim took it in turns to sleep. "You're the ones who'll be doing the fighting. I want you rested!" Mer had commanded.

Storm studied the older girl's face. For the first time since she had known her Mer seemed happy. Suddenly,

Storm realised that she was happy too. Happier than she had been since Dain's death. It felt right, sailing with Mer and Nim, working and planning with them. She missed Scoundrel, but it was better that he stayed safely on Bellum with Linnet. She would, with luck, see the monkey again. If only Nim… But that was asking too much too soon. Maybe once all this was over…

Storm glanced up at the sky and her heart lurched. She looked over the side of the boat. Beneath the water's surface, a dark shape kept pace with them.

"Nim is right." she said quietly. "The Drowned Ones are here. We've found Rekka's island!"

"What?" asked Mer. "How do you know?"

"The Albatross and Dolphin have joined us," Storm said.

"Yes. The Tortoise confirms. We have arrived!" The words were barely out of Nim's mouth when the *Narwhal* climbed the peak of the next wave, and Storm saw the dark outline of an island appear on the horizon. And, between it and them, three raft towns. Peggot had company.

30

Mer's five harriers had followed the *Narwhal* in the hunt for the Drowned Ones, struggling to keep up with the nimble ship and its captain, despite Storm's wind filling their sails. Nim slackened the *Narwhal's* mainsail and the ship slowed. Mer signalled the fleet and the harriers swept past and surged ahead, bounding over the whitecaps in search of their prey.

The *Narwhal* followed, with Mer tacking back and forth, doing her best to hide from the raft towns as she crept towards the solitary island.

Rekka's home, Storm thought. *It really exists.* The Fire-witch's history, told to her over and over during her captivity, had seemed like a tale to frighten children. Yet here was the place where it had all begun. And now Peggot's raft town carried Rekka towards her life's dream of revenge.

The shadow of a giant bird fell over the *Narwhal*. Beneath the water, the shape of a giant dolphin wavered and distorted as it swam alongside the ship. The Elementals had gathered for the final battle. The island, however, drew no closer. Mer gave a frustrated growl as she tacked once again. Nim laughed.

"It's not funny!" Mer exploded. "We're treading water and all the action is happening without us." She gestured towards her harrier ships, which were manoeuvring to form a semicircle round the raft towns.

Nim shrugged. "Many a battle has been lost because of lack of patience. But your people need to move faster! Peggot can't have expected company, or we'd have been spotted by now. If she sees the harriers before they can contain her, she'll run for open sea and it's all to be done again."

As if they had heard his words, the harrier ships changed tack and drove for the raft towns, hulls slapping through the waves, shooting spray into the air.

"Too late!" cried Storm. "They've seen them!"

"That's torn it!" Mer swore creatively as the raft towns headed for open water, racing to avoid being trapped in the shallow waters surrounding the island and its semicircle of reef.

"They're going to get away!" cried Nim.

"No they won't." In Storm's first encounter with Nim's tribe the raft towns had approached Yanlin under cover of a thick fog. Now she began to chant under her breath. She thought of mist and heaviness, of oozing fog. Moisture rose from the sea in blue-white streams, drizzling high into the sky.

The wind stopped so suddenly that Mer swore again as the *Narwhal's* sails emptied, and with a lurch the ship began to drift. "Take in the mainsail!" she growled at Nim, who sprang to the ropes.

Storm ignored everything but dragging water out of the sea and pushing it into the air. She sang softly, quietly, calling on both Dolphin and Albatross. In the space of half a dozen heartbeats the sun had faded to a hazy white ball in the sky, then disappeared entirely. The *Narwhal* floated inside a thick cushion of white. Even the sea itself was invisible.

Sounds were distorted. She heard distant voices crying out in anger and confusion. With each toss of the waves came the clink and jingle of tackle from somewhere unseen, hollow, echoing noises made ghostly by the dead air of the fog.

"That's stopped them getting away," Nim said. "But how does it help us catch Rekka?"

"We don't," Storm said. "You and I will launch the canoe and head for the island. Rekka wants to kill her parents. The best way to stop that is to make sure they aren't on the island when she arrives."

"You're going to leave me here, aren't you?" Mer accused. "Doing nothing while you two have the fun."

"Seems like it," Nim said. "It's a good plan. Don't worry, Mer. We'll be back before you know it. And then you'll have to sail like you never sailed before in your life."

"So we just sail away and leave Rekka unharmed? To start attacking more islands?" Mer's disembodied voice was scathing.

"No," Storm said. "You and Nim get the parents away. I wait for Rekka on the island."

A moment's silence greeted her words.

"You can't face her alone!" Nim exploded.

She couldn't see his face, but his voice told her he was wearing his most stubborn frown.

Mer was silent.

Storm took a breath. "I don't think we have a choice." She waited for someone to argue, to come up with a better plan. But no voice broke the silence of the fog.

$\longleftrightarrow$

The hull of the canoe scraped on the sand and gravel

of an unseen beach, sliding to a juddering halt. Storm expelled the breath she seemed to have been holding forever and leapt over the side into the shallows. She and Nim worked almost soundlessly, using finger jabs and sleeve tugs to communicate as they lifted the canoe and carried it out of reach of the incoming waves.

On land the fog was less thick, but it had been a slow and heart-stopping journey paddling the invisible stretch of water, listening for any hint of hidden Drowned One rafts or harrier ships. When the sound of the water told them they were close to the island, Storm had reached over the bow of the canoe, dropping a sounding rope over and over to avoid holing the canoe on unseen rocks.

"Only you could have got us here," she said to Nim, as they plodded up the beach towards a half-seen fringe of trees. "You really can sail blind."

"I'm a witch," he said. "The earth talks, if you know how to listen. Thank the Tortoise, not me."

She smiled to herself. "I will."

"Halt!" A strange voice called out from the mist directly ahead. "Move one more step and you die!" The last word wobbled fearfully.

Nim had automatically drawn his knife. Now he slipped it back into its scabbard.

"I'm a witch," Storm called. "And so is my friend. We need to speak to your Elders."

"Witches? Here, on Aymai? No one comes here, except a few traders, and them not often. Prove it!"

In answer, Storm pursed her lips and blew gently and steadily. Precise magic was getting easier each time. The mist between them and the hidden speaker lightened and scattered. They stood in a circle of light, the sun shining overhead, while all around them was a thick wall of fog.

Storm saw a thin, stooped man staring at them in amazement, a rusty sword grasped in his shaking hand.

"Is that proof enough? It's my fog, you see. I'm Storm, Weather-witch of Yanlin. And this is Nim, an Earth-witch. We need to talk to your Elders urgently."

"What is all this about?" The man's voice squeaked on the last syllable. "No one comes to Aymai."

"Today's your lucky day, then," said Nim. "There's three raft towns headed right for your island. The Drowned Ones are coming to loot and kill. If you want to live to see another sunrise, I suggest you take us to your Elders. Now."

"Huh?" The man stared at them. He peered at the fog hiding the sea, then slid his sword back into a worn scabbard. "I guess you might as well as talk to them. Drowned Ones?" He shivered and again looked out towards the invisible sea. "Follow me. Drowned Ones! Brrrr." He led them, shuffling and stumbling, up the beach and along a narrow path. They walked beneath trees dripping chilly tears from fog-wet branches.

Buildings reared out of the mist to greet them: low huts, small houses. When their guide reached a huddle of a dozen or so small buildings, he stopped. "This is the village. I'll tell them you're here." He walked to a tall post and tugged on a rope. The iron sound of a bell dinned overhead, its rusty clamour echoing in the fog. "Stay here," said the man. "One of the Elders is deaf. I'll have to fetch him." He trudged off towards a small hut.

Storm pushed the mist away and the sun was soon glaring down on a small, unkempt village. The houses were in poor repair. There were large holes in the bamboo-leaf thatch on several buildings, shutters hanging by leather hinges on others. No Islanders were in sight. She glanced up at the oval of clear sky that opened and saw a speck that must be the Albatross, circling on thermals, high overhead.

"This is the island's main town? It's tiny!" Nim looked around. "And poor. Peggot would take one look and row back out to sea. Wouldn't be worth her time to loot."

"I've never even heard of Aymai," said Storm. "Look, you can see the whole island from this spot. You could walk from one end to the other and be back again between breakfast and lunch."

"This place is on the furthest edge of the Outer Sea," said Nim. "I'd bet they struggle to grow enough crops to feed themselves, let alone trade with other islands. It's incredible they can survive."

Storm shook her head in disbelief. "And this was where Rekka was born? This is the place she's spent a lifetime hating? Hardly seems worth it."

Nim grunted. "They're coming."

The bell had called the villagers of Aymai from their fields and workshops. Soon a scant three dozen Islanders had gathered round them, chatting and muttering and calling questions to each other as they waited for their Elders to assemble. Storm noticed that there were many old people, but few young adults and even fewer children. Everyone was smiling and laughing. They seemed excited, even pleased, to have visitors. At last five elderly people emerged from different buildings and trotted, walked, strolled and shuffled towards the bell post where Storm and Nim waited.

"They won't be so happy when they learn who's out there in the fog," Nim muttered.

"Here we all are!" The stooped man who had brought them to the village reappeared, pulling an elderly man along with him. He pushed the old man into place alongside the other Elders, who had arranged themselves in a semicircle facing their visitors. The youngest, a woman with iron-grey hair in long plaits and a calm face, thudded her Elder staff in the dirt.

"Greetings. Welcome to Aymai. Whalebone tells me you are witches. He said something about Drowned Ones, but he didn't make much sense. Tell me what you know and why you have come to our island."

"It's a long story," Storm said. "I am sorry, but we don't have much time. You are all in danger. There are three Drowned One raft towns out there in the fog."

The news didn't seem to scare her. "Your fog, is it?"

"Mine," Storm said. "But I will have to lift it sometime, and when I do, you will be invaded. Do you have caves, a stronghold, a forest, even, where you can hide?"

"I will hide my people, never fear."

"Good. But there is something else. Someone else. A Fire-witch."

The Elder frowned. For the first time Storm saw

concern enter her eyes. "Has Rekka come, then? Has she returned, as was foretold?"

"You know!"

"I was a young woman. But, yes, we all know the prophecy. I myself witnessed the child's banishment to the cold isle and certain death. The story goes that when the men sailed back to make sure Rekka had perished, they found no bones. Instead, a path of stone led from the banishment place to an island half a day's sail away. It was impossible, yet they swore it was so."

"I have heard the story," Storm said.

"So she comes at last. To destroy our island. To take her revenge."

"Yes."

The Elder bent her head. Keening rose into the hot air like smoke from a fire, as the Islanders began to mourn. Somewhere a funeral drum began to thud, with the soft dead sound of inevitability. It was as though they had long expected this fate – this story, which they had told themselves over and over.

"Where are Rekka's parents?" Storm asked. "I have a plan, but it depends on getting her parents to safety."

The Elder raised her iron-coloured head to stare in amazement at Storm. "But they are dead. They died years ago. Long years ago. When I was still young.

They died the first monsoon season after their daughter disappeared. The fever was bad that year."

Storm stared at her, mouth open in shock. Rekka was coming to murder parents who had been dead since she first plotted her fiery revenge. This changed everything!

←——————→

"They are buried here." The Elder pointed to a dusty, narrow cave opening in the cliff near the harbour path. "Our Ancestor cave."

"What were their names?" Storm asked.

"Fin was the father. A hard man, sharp like his name. And the mother was called Mayna. She was a gentle, kind girl. Younger than me. But from the day she was married, she stopped smiling." The Elder sighed. "Life has always been hard here. And then the prophecy broke her heart. She loved her child. I think she welcomed the fever that took her to the next world. She thought the child had died, you see, and that they would be together in the land of the Ancestors. Huh!" The woman shook her head. "Life makes fools of us all. Poor Mayna."

Storm threw a look at Nim, who was shuffling his feet impatiently. He looked at her meaningfully. Time was short.

"Elder," Storm said gently but firmly, "there is no time to waste. You must get your people into hiding. Keep them away from the village. I will lift the fog as soon as my friend here is back on our ship, and then Rekka will come."

"No," Nim interrupted. "I told you. I'm not leaving you here on your own to fight Rekka. It took both of us last time."

"This isn't last time. I need you to stop Peggot and the others landing warriors. Rekka is bound to be in the first boat. That first boat is the only one I want to land on Aymai! You have to get to Mer as quickly as you can and tell her the plan. It will take all of you, all the harriers, to keep Peggot busy."

Nim opened his mouth. Shut it. Turned and ran for the harbour.

"He worries for you," said the Elder.

Storm nodded. She watched the woman hustle away to shepherd her people to safety, and turned to walk down to the harbour after Nim. Soon it would be time. Rekka was coming home.

31

Storm lay in the waist-high grass on the cliff top above the small harbour. She watched a canoe power through the surf towards the lonely island of Aymai. It held three people. One of them was the Fire-witch.

Once the villagers were safe, she had chosen her reconnaissance spot and begun counting her heartbeats. The plan was to give Nim and Mer enough time to get their ships far enough out to sea to set an ambush. When she had counted to five hundred, Storm had released the fog. In the space of a few breaths the heavy, damp whiteness had evaporated in the heat, and the sun had once more sparkled on the whitecaps beyond the curve of the island's breakwater.

Three raft towns had been prowling just outside the harbour. Beyond them, three or four bowshots further out to sea, Storm had spotted the *Narwhal* and the Bellum harriers. She had clenched her hands tight as she waited for Peggot's decision. Would the Drowned One give chase? Retreat? Or go ahead and land Rekka? And who would accompany the witch? A dozen Drowned One warriors would more than complicate things.

Storm had staked everything on the Fire-witch demanding to be put ashore no matter what. Peggot would be worried about the harriers attacking, but this close to Aymai, Rekka would surely be maddened by the lust for revenge. Even Peggot might not want to risk thwarting a madwoman!

Storm had groaned with relief when she saw that her gamble had paid off. First, she had heard distant orders shouted, then the clink of tackle and slap of a boat dropping on to water. And then a canoe – a small one, praise the Ancestors! – had rounded the side of the nearest raft town and struck out for shore.

Now two figures bent over oars, rowing strongly as the canoe drove through the turbulence of the breakwater into Aymai's placid harbour. The third person in the prow of the canoe sat motionless, her red tunic a shriek of anger against the blue-green water.

When the canoe slid on to the sand of the beach,

the Fire-witch waited for one of the warriors to splash to her side. Rekka scrambled on to his shoulders and, riding a Drowned One piggyback, returned to her island.

Once clear of the tide, the Fire-witch leapt on to the sandy shore. Had it been Storm's imagination, or had the earth of Aymai shuddered the instant Rekka's feet touched it? She raised herself to crouching, making sure to keep well hidden in the sharp-edged marram grass, and watched Rekka trudge through the sand towards the village path without a backward glance at her companions, who remained with the canoe.

The Drowned One who had carried Rekka to shore made a gesture to ward off evil at her back. Then the men pushed their canoe into the water and returned to the waiting raft towns. It was even better than Storm had dared hope: Rekka wanted every death on Aymai to be at her hands! It made things simpler, but as Storm examined her plan doubt grew in her mind. The Albatross and Dolphin had vanished. And as for the Tortoise… Storm pushed thoughts of Nim from her mind. She was on her own this time. She would do her best, and that, Dain had always said, was all anyone could do.

She caught up with the Fire-witch in the village.

Thinner than ever, a spear of a woman dressed in a blood-red tunic that hung, shapeless, from bony shoulders, Rekka stood with her back to Storm. The Fire-witch was motionless. She did not turn her head as Storm drew near. She seemed lost in a dream, or deep in thought. The silence was brooding, like the still before a thunderstorm.

Storm waited. She knew the woman had heard her approach. Her heart was thudding: she was still frightened of Rekka. The temptation to attack now, when her enemy's back was to her, was strong. But that was not why the Elementals had lent her their power. That was not what her mother's spirit expected, as it waited for her in the land of the Ancestors.

"Hello, Storm," Rekka said at last. Her voice was different. It was a brittle crunch: like charcoal being broken with a mallet. When the witch turned to face her, Storm could not stop herself gasping.

"Not a pretty sight, am I?" Rekka said with a mocking smile, and Storm swallowed. It was true. The magma had wrought fearsome changes. The Fire-witch's magic had cost her dear.

The woman looking at Storm was bald – her scorched hair had not grown back. Her broken arm wore a splint wrapped in dirty bandages. Her skin was still the strange grey-tan it had turned after their duel. And her eyes stared out of a face that had collapsed into a net of wrinkles – it was the face of a very old woman, not one in middle age. That she was unwell was clear; her breathing was rasping and uneven. The Fire-witch had asked too much of her human body.

"You are dying," Storm said and felt a sudden, surprising sadness. The little girl of Rekka's story lived inside Storm's imagination. She would never be free of her.

"I have enough life left to destroy this place," snarled the Fire-witch. "I should have guessed you would figure out my intention; you're a clever opponent. But I never thought you would find your way here before me. I made sure never to foul my lips with its name."

"Aymai. You should say it. You should say their names: Fin and Mayna."

Rekka stiffened. "You dare?"

"I've come to show you where they are buried."

The stillness grew until it became more than stillness. It swelled into timeless horror. And loss. Such loss. Watching Rekka's face contort with the child's loss of its parents, the adolescent's loss of grace, the adult's loss of hope, Storm felt her own loss – of Dain, of her father, of Thorn – swell up inside her with pain as sharp as birth, as remorseless as death.

The woman staggered, then pushed herself straight again. "Show me."

It was a slow, painful journey to Aymai's cave of the Ancestors. Rekka trudged behind Storm, her feet scuffing the earth. Sometimes the Fire-witch paused to catch her breath. Storm did not dare to offer her a shoulder to lean on. Instead, she found a straight branch half decapitated by a wind storm, twisted it free and handed it to the witch, who took it without a word or nod of thanks.

Rekka stood for a long time in front of the cave, staring at its dark mouth. She did not go inside. "Tell me."

"They died that year. The year you were sent into the cold. Fever took them."

"How do you know their names?"

"The chief Elder – she remembered them. And you. She was younger than Mayna. She said, and I have no reason to disbelieve her, that your mother loved you."

"She never smiled. I don't ever remember her smiling at me."

"Do you remember her loving you?"

A grunt of pain. A hacking cough. "She let them do it."

"Yes. She couldn't save you. And after that she welcomed death when the fever came."

"No one. Only the Salamander!" The Fire-witch drew a deep rasping breath, let it out in a puff of smoke and steam. She turned a long dragon face to stare at Storm. "I will destroy this island. I will kill its people. I will destroy you." Rekka grinned. She licked bloodless lips with a thin leathery tongue, and Storm felt her stomach turn over. The Fire-witch seemed inhuman. If that was true, she had lost her gamble, and Aymai would be the final battleground of the Elementals.

Rekka crowed with laughter. "Look!" the witch cried, and pointed towards the crumbling hill at the heart of the island, the cone of a long-dead volcano. Smoke – dirty black, brown and green smoke – clawed its way out of the tree tops before bubbling into the sky. Suddenly, the earth shook and, accompanied by the rumbling roar of a subterranean inferno, a finger of flame shot from the now active volcano.

Storm stared, aghast. "No!"

"See, Weather-witch?" Rekka's words exploded into the air, full of threat. The witch was transformed. She had cast aside her stick. Her skin glowed orange. In her eyes danced devil flames. "The Salamander makes me strong again. I am invincible! And I shall start the

261

killing with you!" The Fire-witch raised her hand to strike.

"Are you such a fool?" Storm made herself laugh in Rekka's startled face.

This was it. The moment. Everything depended on her next few words.

"Haven't you figured it out? The Salamander betrayed you twice over! Do you still do its bidding?"

There was a stunned silence. She could almost see Rekka rejecting her words, refusing to understand them. Then ... slowly, understanding dawned. And still the Fire-witch struggled to escape the knowledge that gripped her.

"Liar!" shouted Rekka. But she lowered her arm. "What do you mean? Tell me!"

"It knew," said Storm. "Of course the Salamander knew! Your parents were dead before the Fire spirit rescued you, but it didn't bother to tell you that one important fact. It kept you ignorant on purpose.

"The Salamander needed you to hate your parents. It made you waste your life dreaming of revenge against people who were already dead! *That* is how much the Salamander loves you! Fire stole your life so it could feed you the poison of hate and turn you into its monster. And still, like some cringing puppy, you return to lick the hand of the one who has cheated you?"

The Fire-witch stared at her. Slowly, the fire in her pupils dwindled. Rekka said, her voice crunching and ugly, "If there is nothing left, why should I not destroy this place? If killing is all that I am good for, death is all I have."

Storm answered from her heart. If this was not truth, then she knew nothing at all and her entire life had been a lie. Dain's face filled her mind's eye as she spoke. "Because your mother, Mayna, loved you. Hate her if you must, for not being able to protect you. But she died loving you. She died hoping to see you in the land of the Ancestors. What will you do, Rekka?"

The woman stood a long time, thinking. Then, slowly, painfully, she bent down and picked up her discarded walking stick. As she did so, the island shook again, and Storm heard the scream of trees being ripped from the earth. Orange as the sun at sunset, a glow-worm trail of fire wriggled free of the earth and began to burn its way down the hillside towards the village.

"You see," said the woman. "The Salamander will have death." She began to trudge up the path, towards the cone of the newborn volcano. "Come with me," Rekka said without turning round. Storm followed.

With each step they took the island shuddered more

violently as the Salamander worked to tear it apart, forcing fire through the helpless earth. Overhead, mag-mag monkeys screamed and fled, leaping from tree to tree as ash and fire began to flow down the hillside. The air was full of screeching birds taking wing. Storm watched them helplessly. If the Salamander sank this island, the animals and even the birds would perish; there was no land near enough to swim or fly to.

The woman stumped on, seeming not to notice the panicked wildlife racing down the hill past them. She climbed, breath rasping louder and louder, until at last the path reached a high cliff. Here Rekka stood, at the edge of the sky, staring out to sea. Storm came as close as she dared. The cliff was sheer and smooth, tumbling down to a tiny cove where the waves churned endlessly against the rock, splashing spray high into the air. A small rainbow hung in the mist, so close it looked like you could step out and walk on its shimmering colours.

"This was my mother's favourite place," Rekka said. "She brought me here most days. She would hold me in her arms. She never said anything. She never smiled. But she held me close."

The woman turned to Storm. "It won't stop. Don't think you've won. This is just one battle in an eternity.

Tell them. Make them remember. The Salamander will come again." She reached out and laid a withered, hot hand against Storm's cheek. "You were the lucky one. I do not grudge you your good fortune. Remember me, Storm."

Before she could recoil from the touch of Rekka's hand, before she could understand the intent behind the words, the woman who had been the Salamander's dragon turned and leapt from the cliff.

She fell silently. Swiftly. Tumbling over and over, straight as the stick she still held in an outstretched hand, until she plunged into the sea and was gone.

Storm shivered with shock. Grief surprised her and she bit her lip to keep from crying out.

I Chose badly. I will do better next time.

The voice flickered. It seethed inside Storm's head. She had hoped never to hear its poisonous tones again. She turned and, for the first time in her life, Storm saw the Salamander, the Elemental spirit of Fire.

It crouched, smoking and stinking, on a patch of hillside near the path. The ground where it stood was charred black. The Elemental was as beautiful as it was fearsome. It was clothed in scales that shone like gold and red rubies. Fire flickered over its body, blue, red, white. Its eyes were large and mesmerising. They swirled like a child's pinwheel. Storm dared one glance at them, then, sick and giddy, looked carefully over its head.

I offer you one last chance to accept me, said the Fire Elemental. *Refuse, and you die where you stand!*

"Perhaps," said Storm.

She looked up at the sky to see enormous wings sweeping towards them. She looked out to sea to see the Dolphin leap as high as the island's ancient volcano and descend again into the sea without a ripple or splash. She glanced back towards the Salamander and saw the hill behind the spirit swell into the shape of a Tortoise of immense size. It pushed itself from the earth on clawed feet, lifting its heavy shell. Its long neck swivelled, and she looked into the ancient eyes of the Earth spirit and was awed.

Storm clouds gathered. Rain fell in torrents from the sky, like the first downpours of a monsoon. Storm was drenched to the skin in a heartbeat. She shouted with joy: "You have lost, Salamander! The Balance is maintained. Your war will not happen!"

She pointed out to sea, where the retreating raft towns were mere specks in the far distance. The five harrier ships bobbed, resting at anchor. Beside them swam the *Narwhal*. A canoe was sweeping past the breakwater towards shore, the two people in it paddling furiously. Nim and Mer. Her friends were coming.

When she turned back, the Fire Elemental had vanished. A few last wisps of sulphur-tainted smoke drifted into the sky from the dead volcano and were swept away by the wind.

It took all her diving skill. It took many attempts over the rest of that long day. But she found Rekka's body at last, at the bottom of the cove, tangled in weed. Her lungs burning for want of air, Storm tugged and pulled until the sea gave up its prize. Kicking for her life, she towed the dead witch after her up into the air.

Nim helped her haul the dead woman ashore, helped her carry the corpse up to the island's lonely Ancestor cave. But it was Aymai's Elder, the grey-haired woman, who helped Storm bathe and dry Rekka's body, dress her in scarlet, and carry her inside the cave to lie beside her parents.

Storm stood looking down at Rekka for a long time, but there were no answers to be found in the dead face. She only knew that it had taken more courage than she could imagine for her enemy to plunge from the cliff. Rekka had feared water more than death itself.

Storm sighed. She took off the gold bangle on her

right wrist, exposing the scar that was the result of the Salamander's first attack on her life. She slid the bangle on to the bony, frail wrist of the dead woman – the only grave gift she had to offer. It glittered in the light of the oil lamp.

"I will tell them," Storm said to Rekka. "I will make them remember. You will not be forgotten."

She left the cave. The silvering moonlight seemed bright after the darkness. She smiled at Nim and Mer, who had waited for her as the sun set. One of them had a home to return to but no parents. One had a home that needed putting right, and a mother who might never be right. One had no home and no parents. But Rekka had told the truth. They were the fortunate ones. They had friends and allies. They had a future.

As she followed her friends down the hill towards the village, rest and food, and preparations for tomorrow's journey back to Yanlin, Storm gave thanks to the Ancestors. Silently, she said goodbye to the Albatross, Dolphin and Tortoise, wondering if she would meet them again in the future, in a place and time as yet unknown, in a story yet to be told.

Acknowledgements

My gratitude to the team at Nosy Crow for their general brilliance and the best covers of my career. Special thanks goes to my editor, Kirsty Stansfield; to my agent, Jenny Savill of Andrew Nurnberg Associates; and to friends and family.

I thank my mother, Darlene Bryson Renner, who died in 2019, for a lifetime of support and encouragement. She loved these books. I have no Ancestor cave, but The Drowned Ones is my grave gift to her memory.

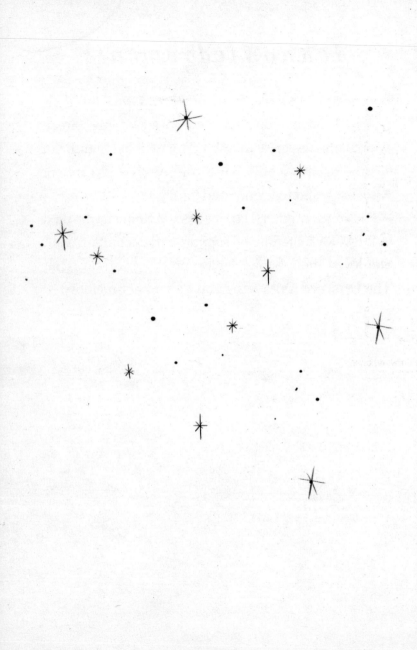